He couldn't possibly know

Anna balled her hand a
hadn't captured her fist and h
not up for discussion."

"Where it concerns Sandra it is. You weren't seeing anyone, so why all of a sudden are you going out? What's going on?"

"How do you know I wasn't dating someone?"

"I checked you out—thoroughly."

Stunned, she sat on the couch which she instantly decided was a mistake when Ian eased down next to her. "I'm not a suspect."

"When I work with someone, I find out everything I can about that person. No surprises."

"Everything?" she murmured, wondering if he knew her secret that she had worked hard to hide from others.

He nailed her beneath a penetratingly intense look. "Yes, everything, Anna. I know about your abilities."

To all the paranormal romance readers
Thank you for your support.

DREAM SNATCHER

* * *

Shauna Michaels

ImaJinn
Books

DREAM SNATCHER
Published by ImaJinn Books, a division of ImaJinn

Copyright ©2002 by Margaret Daley
Printed and bound in the United States of America. All rights reserved. No part of this book may be reproduced in any form or by any means (electronic, mechanical, photocopying, recording, or otherwise) without prior written permission of both the copyright holder and the above publisher of this book, except by a reviewer, who may quote brief passages in a review. For information, address: ImaJinn Books, a division of ImaJinn, P.O. Box 162, Hickory Corners, MI 49060-0162; or call toll free 1-877-625-3592.

ISBN: 1-893896-76-5

10 9 8 7 6 5 4 3 2 1

PUBLISHER'S NOTE:
This book is a work of fiction. Names, characters, places and incidents are products of the author's imagination or are used fictitiously. Any resemblance to actual events or locales or persons, living or dead, is entirely coincidental.

Books are available at quantity discounts when used to promote products or services. For information please write to: Marketing Division, ImaJinn Books, P.O. Box 162, Hickory Corners, MI 49060-0162, or call toll free 1-877-625-3592.

Cover design by Patricia Lazarus

ImaJinn Books, a division of ImaJinn
P.O. Box 162, Hickory Corners, MI 49060-0162
Toll Free: 1-877-625-3592
http://www.imajinnbooks.com

One

Her cry of ecstasy pierced the still night. Mind-shattering pleasure hurled her through space. She clung to him and cried out again. His own release shuddered through her, fragmenting her into a hundred different pieces.

When she returned to reality, all energy drained from her, she curled up against his hard body and welcomed the blissful serenity of sleep. Never had she reached such fulfillment, she thought as a heavy fog blanketed her mind. It was as though he'd come into her body and become a part of her.

In the dark he watched her close her eyes and her breathing slow to the steady even pace of deep slumber. He placed his hand over her breast, the beat of her heart strong. Her essence surged into his fingertips.

She would give him many hours of pleasure. The wait had been worth it, he thought, hovering over her as though he was a predator waiting to strike his prey. He smiled at that analogy because in truth he was.

When she sank completely into the realm of dreams, he closed his eyes and cradled her head, pausing to savor the blissful moment. His spirit lifted and flowed through his fingers into her. He honed in on her reserve of energy. His soared as he siphoned hers. His power matched then eclipsed hers, driving her toward the dark void.

Suddenly she moaned, shifting beneath his hands. She

was stronger than most, her life forces struggling to break free of his hold. He focused totally on her, fusing his core with hers and demanding her submission. She arched one final time, then went limp in his hands.

His cry of ecstasy pierced the still night as he melded with her. Her thoughts and memories poured into him and swirled about in his mind, becoming his. Through the blissful euphoria a beacon glowed, drawing him in.

He rolled off her and sat up, his back to her. A smile slithered across his face as he mulled over the new bit of information he'd gleaned from her mind. So her sister was stronger, more talented, a better feed.

He threw back his head and laughed, the sound echoing through the silent chamber. Her sister would be perfect as his next conquest.

***

I'm coming for you.

Alarm slammed into her. Anna Stanfield bolted up in her bed. Sweat drenched her nightgown, the cotton fabric clinging to her body. Pressing her hand to her breast, she drew in gulps of air to still the pounding of her heart. Slowly, its beating returned to normal as she took in her surroundings. Her bedroom. Near dawn. Everything in its place. Just a dream. Nothing more.

Tossing back the covers, Anna slipped from her bed and padded to the window overlooking her garden. Her pink tulips beckoned in the gray dawn. Fingers of sunlight fanned upward, coloring the sky in blinding crimson and gold. She loved this time of day best.

Then why do I feel so cold, as though someone has invaded me?

Anna hugged her arms to herself and stepped back from the window. The uncanny feeling someone was watching her gripped her in its talons.

Two

He stood at the redwood railing staring down into the valley far below, his sharp eyes taking in the gray rabbit scurrying for cover and the fox trotting across the meadow, nearly hidden in the tall grass. Wind whipped his long hair about his face, the chill of the mountain air carried on it. But he didn't feel the cold. He didn't feel anything. He'd stopping feeling a long time ago—hundreds of years before.

He'd seen everything there was to see many times over. He only had one purpose in his life now—to protect his people. His hand clenched about the wooden railing as thoughts of the Chameleon ran rampant through his mind. He'd stop him this time. He would use anyone or any means to accomplish that goal. The Chameleon was jeopardizing their very existence, and that would not be allowed.

"Hawk, it's time. Everyone is assembled and waiting for you."

He nodded and turned away from the railing. With economical strides he quickly covered the distance to the council chamber. Scanning the eight men and women sitting at the round table, Hawk eased into the only empty chair in the darkened room. Books graced the floor to ceiling shelves along three of the walls. Mounted on the fourth wall was a large television screen that was hooked directly into a computer system. At the moment the screen was blank except for the word, "Circle."

"Can you give us an update on the Chameleon?" the only man in the room who looked over fifty asked.

"There's another victim, a woman named Sandra Stanfield," Hawk answered his uncle.

"Are you sure it's the Chameleon?" A woman with striking white hair and a youthful face poured a glass of spring water and downed several swallows, her blue eyes riveted to Hawk.

"Yes, it's him. But he may have made a mistake this time. This is the second victim in the same area."

"He's getting bolder, and with each killing we risk exposure. We can't have that." A woman in her late twenties, beautiful in a cold kind of way, stood. Her tension was conveyed in the rigid lines of her body as she leaned into the large, round oak table and gripped it.

"Dolphin, take a seat. Let Hawk explain what he plans to do next," the white haired woman said in a soothing voice.

"But the Chameleon has eluded him for years. These latest incidents are generating some interest among the humans."

Hawk rose slowly and with such control that every member of the Circle looked at him, waiting for him to speak. His gaze shifted around the table, his mind touching each person in the room, his thoughts brushing across theirs but going no farther than the surface of their minds.

Dolphin sat again, her tension melting under Hawk's silent reassurances. Her regard fell under his unrelenting one, and she murmured, "I was just concerned because the world has changed a lot since we first came here. Now news travels instantly from one continent to another. It is harder and harder to keep secrets."

"Remember who I am in the human world. I have control over the situation and what information is available. These murders won't be linked. Have I ever let the Circle down?" Hawk asked, his voice rough, cold around the edges.

"No," the white haired woman said.

"Since my father's death, I've been the Protector. I'll take care of the Chameleon. You have my word no one will stand in my way of capturing him and bringing him to justice—our kind of justice."

"That is all we need to know. I think we can move along to the other business." The oldest member of the council shuffled through a stack of papers before him. "Has Dove reported in about the uprising in Southeast Asia? Was she able to get close to the rebel leader to influence him?"

***

Anna shifted at the podium, her feet killing her. Next time she would wear sensible shoes, she decided, scanning the audience for any more raised hands.

"I have time for one more question," she said and pointed to a young man in the back row.

As she dropped her arm back to her side, a thought nibbled at her mind, forging its way past her barriers. Instinctively, she shut down, but the thought shoved past her defenses.

Your sister is in grave danger. Anna surveyed the people in the audience, a tremor rippling down her length.

The college student she'd chosen rose. "Dr. Stanfield, how do you account for women's intuition, then?"

Resolved not to give in to her exhaustion, Anna pushed away the uneasy sensation that someone was in her mind. Impossible. She never played mind games, even with herself. Of course her sister was in trouble. She was in the hospital in a coma. That was a fact manifesting itself in her weary thoughts as someone's communication.

"Dr. Stanfield?"

Her painful grip on the podium anchored her in the present. "Women's intuition certainly isn't an extrasensory perception. I think some people, men call it hunches, know how to read others better and pick up on subtle nuances when most of us don't." Anna closed the folder that held her lecture notes, her composure firmly in place.

Are you so sure about that?

She blinked and scanned the crowd of college students, but most of them were getting ready to leave, a few even standing.

Anna shook off the feeling of foreboding. The exhaustion of the past few days played havoc with her judgment. "Please read the next chapter in the book. My next lecture will cover the brain." Several of her students moaned, and she added, "I realize this subject isn't as exciting as psychotic behavior, ESP or the human sexual drive, but the brain is what controls us. And we're just beginning to understand its complexities."

Her students filed past her as she stuffed her notes into her briefcase and prepared to follow. She would ignore the fact that her hands trembled and chalk it up to exhaustion, too. She didn't have the energy or time to have a mental breakdown. Hearing voices in her head, indeed.

Anna started for the door. She was late. She hoped traffic wasn't too bad. Glancing at her watch, she knew she wouldn't make it to the hospital when the doctor made his rounds if she didn't get lucky and hit every light just right.

"Dr. Stanfield, may I have a moment of your time?"

Irritated by the interruption, she turned toward the deep masculine voice and started to tell the man no. Instead she found herself stopping and staring at him—or rather into dark eyes that were almost midnight black, eyes that spoke of having seen too much violence. A flutter danced down her spine. "Yes?"

"You're a psychologist, and yet you insist ESP isn't possible."

"Your question being?"

"How do you explain some of the data your fellow colleagues are gathering concerning extrasensory perception?"

She drew herself up straighter, ignoring the danger signals emanating from this stranger, and answered, "I never said it wasn't possible. I just need sound scientific data before I buy into it."

"Then you don't deny there are many mysteries where the mind is involved?"

"No. I'd be a fool if I thought otherwise. Good day." She pivoted toward the door, but his next words froze her.

"I'm investigating your sister's case."

"My sister's case? There is no case. Who are you?"

"I work for the FBI. I'm Ian McGregory." He retrieved his wallet from the inside of his black suit coat and flipped it open to reveal his identification.

"The FBI? I don't understand. My sister is in a coma at the hospital, and I'm late as it is to meet with her doctor." She again looked at her watch to emphasize the point.

"I've been following a series of cases where women have either ended up in a coma or dead, and the doctors can't explain why."

"You think it's murder?"

"Yes, I do. There's a pattern to the deaths."

Murder? Stunned, Anna grasped the edge of the podium to keep herself from collapsing. She felt as though her world had been turned upside down. A few days ago a friend of her sister's had discovered Sandra unconscious on her bed, and now this man was telling her it was attempted murder. "I can't imagine anyone wanting to kill my sister."

"Sometimes there isn't a reason—at least one you or I can understand."

"I'm sorry I can't be of much help. My sister and I weren't that close. Our lives went in different directions." She heard the regret in her voice and prayed she had an opportunity to change that when her sister recovered.

"Had you talked to her lately?"

"A week ago. She was excited about a new man in her life."

Ian straightened, his gaze sharpening. "Who?"

Anna shrugged. "She didn't say. She never talked about the men she was dating. At least not to me." She regretted that now, too, realizing that Sandra and she avoided each other because they made each other uncomfortable.

"So you know nothing about this man. How long they dated? His name? What he did for a living? Has he been to the hospital to see your sister?"

Anna shook her head in answer to each question, suddenly realizing how strange it was that Sandra's latest man hadn't come to the hospital to check on her condition. "I did get the feeling they hadn't been dating long, maybe a few times. Do you think he might have something to do with Sandra being in a coma? They don't even know why she's in one. They've ruled out drugs, brain injury, all the usual suspects. How could this man be responsible?" Anna was beginning to doubt this FBI agent knew what he was talking about, and she needed him to be wrong because the alternative meant that someone had tried to kill her younger sister.

"I'm investigating every possibility, even this mysterious boyfriend of your sister's."

Anna released her grip on the podium. "I must go. I'm sorry I couldn't be of any help." She headed for the double doors, needing to put some distance between herself and the FBI agent. He made her uncomfortable. Or rather the subject he wanted to talk about did.

Ian fell into step next to her. "Mind if I tag along? I'd like to hear what your sister's doctor has to say."

"What if I said yes I minded?"

"I'd come anyway." He smiled at her. "Part of my job. Sorry."

"Then I guess I don't mind."

His smile was warm, easing the sharp lines of his face into an almost pleasant countenance. He wasn't the most handsome man she'd ever seen, but his hard looks were strangely pleasing to the eye. She noted his black hair was longer than she would have thought an FBI agent would wear, but then she didn't know any other agents to compare him to. His dark suit did little to hide his muscular build, indicating he was in top physical form.

In the parking lot he stopped at the car next to hers. "I'll follow you to St. John's."

The thought of his car parked next to hers in the university's large lot sent another shiver through her. She pushed the feeling to the background. More and more lately she'd been getting these weird sensations at odd times. She didn't want them. They only caused trouble.

What about your dream last night? What about waking up in a cold sweat this morning? Anna determinedly pushed those questions away, too. Exhaustion was the only answer she would accept. Ever since her sister had gone into a deep coma, Anna hadn't slept more than a few hours at a time.

In her car she took a moment to compose herself and place a tight rein on her emotions. Could this FBI agent be right? Could someone have tried to murder Sandra?

For a few seconds panic seized her. She felt herself fighting for her life, struggling to retain the forces within her body. Then everything went blank, leaving her drained. Sagging forward, she rested her forehead against the steering wheel and drew in deep breaths. Her heart raced, her pulse thundered in her ears. Dizziness attacked her senses, making the world tilt at an odd angle.

Oh, Lord, it has begun again.

A knock on her window startled her. She shrank back at the same time she twisted toward the sound. Removing his dark sunglasses that completely hid his eyes, Ian McGregory stared at her, concern in his expression. Anna started the engine and pushed the button to lower the window.

He leaned against the car. "Are you all right? You look like you've seen a ghost."

"Yes—yes. I'm fine. Just tired. I haven't had much sleep since Sandra got sick."

"Why don't you let me drive you to the hospital?"

"No, I'm fine really."

"You're pale. Your hands are shaking. You don't look fine."

"Gee a gal likes to hear that." She attempted a smile that faltered immediately. Clasping her hands around the steering wheel to keep them from trembling, she added, "I appreciate the offer, but no thanks."

He started to argue with her but instead turned away and walked to the driver's side of his car. Her deep sigh of relief blew out from between pursed lips. On the short drive to the hospital she was determined to get herself under firm control. She had this awful feeling she was going to need that in the next few hours. She'd spent a good part of her life perfecting an iron grip over her emotions, and she wasn't going to lose it now in front of a stranger.

At the hospital, Anna deliberately squeezed into a tight space between two cars so that Mr. McGregory had to park several rows away. She smiled, thinking it was ridiculous to feel she had to exert a show of independence to the FBI agent, no matter how small the gesture was. Leaving her car, she hurried toward the building without waiting for him.

Ian caught up with her at the bank of elevators. He slanted her a look, then faced the opening doors. On the ride up, silence reigned in the car, except for the occasional ding as they passed a floor. Anna sensed the man's gaze on the back of her head as she tapped her foot, waiting for the doors to open. For a few seconds she felt as if he had reached inside her mind. She immediately, instinctively, threw up a wall, then realized she was being ridiculous, just as she had been in the lecture hall earlier. His assertion of attempted murder was making her edgy, causing her to do and think things she normally wouldn't.

When they reached Sandra's room, Anna blocked the entrance. "I'd like to see my sister alone—please."

He folded his arms across his chest and leaned against the wall. "I'll wait out here for the doctor."

Anna went into her sister's hospital room, pausing by the doorway. Every time she saw Sandra lying in the bed, her white-blond hair almost fading against the stark white sheets, Anna had to fight the helplessness rising in her. She wanted to do something for her sister, but there was nothing she could do.

Finally she moved to Sandra's side and took her hand as she did whenever she visited. "Sandra, you're looking better today," she said in the most cheerful voice she could muster. If her sister somehow could hear her, Anna wanted to give her a reason to wake up.

"I came from class." Anna scooted a hardback chair closer. "You know those new shoes I bought last week that I told you about yesterday? Well, I wore them today, and after fifteen minutes teaching my class, I thought my feet were going to go numb. In fact, I'm going to take them off right now." She slipped out of her shoes and welcomed the coolness of the tile floor against her stocking-clad feet.

She began to tell Sandra about the lecture she'd given her students about maintaining the integrity of lab experiments. The whole time she spoke, she continued to hold Sandra's hand as though she could will life back into her body and would give anything if she could. So intent was she on doing the impossible that she didn't hear anyone come in until someone cleared his throat.

She peered over her shoulder at Ian McGregory and Dr. Nelson, who stood next to him. After gently releasing Sandra's hand and laying it on top of the sheet over her stomach, Anna stood. "Have you found anything yet, doctor?"

"No, nothing new to indicate what could have caused this coma. Most puzzling."

Anna frowned. This was what she had heard for the past few days. "Then you have no idea when or if she'll come out of it?"

"No." Dr. Nelson scribbled some notes on the chart he held.

"What are her vital signs, her brain activity levels?"

Ian McGregory's question reinforced why the FBI man was standing in her sister's hospital room. Anna wanted to shout her rejection of his claim that Sandra had been a victim of some sinister man who was running around murdering innocent women. But what if she had been?

Dr. Nelson looked from Ian to Anna. "I'm not—"

"It's okay to answer him, Dr. Nelson. This is Ian McGregory with the FBI."

"FBI?"

"Yes, he feels Sandra might have met with foul play."

"I suppose that's possible, but not likely. There are no

signs of foul play."

"What do her brain scans show?"

"The lowest levels she can have and still be considered alive."

Anna sucked in a deep breath. She knew this, had heard it before, but she felt hopelessness every time she thought about how precarious Sandra's hold was on life. It was as if they were biding their time until her younger sister just slipped away.

After the doctor left, a tension-fraught silence descended. Anna and Ian stood on opposite sides of the hospital bed, Sandra lying between them. Again the dark intensity of his eyes drew Anna's gaze to him. She was acutely aware of her heart beating against her breast, of each breath she inhaled, as if her bodily functions were magnified in her mind.

Then one corner of his mouth lifted, and he broke visual contact with her. He looked down at Sandra. "I wish she could tell us what happened," he murmured in the quiet of the room.

"What do you think she would say?" Anna asked, still not convinced this man knew what he was talking about.

"Who did this to her. Who she was with when this happened."

"So you still believe this was attempted murder?"

His regard captured hers. "Yes."

Anna sank down onto the hardback chair, her legs weak, and grasped her trembling hands in her lap. The clasp of her interlaced fingers tightened until her knuckles whitened. "Has this happened to anyone else here in Lexington?"

"There was a coed who died a few months back, and the cause of death was never determined. The medical examiner said her heart just stopped beating."

"I remember that young girl. She was a premed

student." A strong urge to connect with her sister caused Anna to take Sandra's hand again. "You said something about other women in comas?"

"Actually, Sandra's only the third woman I've found who has been left in a coma."

"What happened to the other women? Are they still alive?"

"No."

That one word slammed into her as though he'd pealed a death toll. "How long were the other women in a coma?"

"A few days."

Anna's grip on Sandra tensed. "What did their doctors say?"

"The same thing. They couldn't find a reason for them to be in a coma. When they died the autopsy revealed nothing, either."

Anna closed her eyes and wished this would all go away. A sense of panic invaded her, taking her by surprise. The alien feeling was gone before she could grab hold of it. Her eyes bolted open, and she stared at her sister, who looked so peaceful. Sandra's thin features were relaxed, her dark, long lashes brushing the tops of her pale cheeks.

Dropping Sandra's hand, Anna severed her connection to her sister. She hugged herself, a chill embedding itself deep inside her.

"Are you all right?"

She'd forgotten for a moment that he was in the room with her. How could she? His presence dominated the small space and charged the air. "You seem to be making a regular habit of asking me that."

"This can't be easy for you. How about some lunch? My treat."

She thought about turning him down, but something in his expression persuaded her otherwise. "Okay. I'm not sure I'm very hungry, though." She put her high heels back on, smoothed her black, straight skirt and rose.

"Then keep me company." Ian came around the bed. "I'll even let you pick the restaurant, since I'm new in town."

He casually touched the small of her back as they were walking from the room. A jolt like an electrical current flashed up her spine. She quickly stepped away. Nonplused by the physical contact, she slanted a look at him and wondered again if she was falling apart, imagining things that weren't there.

Outside in the parking lot he paused next to her car. "I'll follow you to the restaurant."

"What do you like to eat?"

"Surprise me."

"Somehow I get the feeling you aren't a man who likes to be surprised."

"But in this case I'll be relatively safe."

Safe. Anna thought about that word as she drove to a little cafe near the university that she frequented for lunch. Sandra should have been safe. Her lifestyle as a university librarian certainly didn't call attention to her. She'd led a quiet, productive life, often immersed in some book. Who would possibly want to harm her little sister?

Ian met her at the door into Molly's Cafe and opened it for her. She proceeded into the restaurant, again a sharp awareness of his gaze on her as she weaved her way to an empty table. She was sure nothing escaped this man, that he was attentive to everything going on around him.

"Is this a student hangout?" he asked, taking the chair facing the large picture window that overlooked the busy street.

"Some of the older students like to come here, but mostly professors meet here. The food's good and reasonably priced. And best of all, Molly, who owns this cafe, doesn't mind us lingering over our meal. We have had some interesting discussions here that have gone on half the afternoon."

"Academically stimulating?"

"More thought-provoking than anything. David Pierce, a friend of mine in the Philosophy Department, can get a person thinking about an aspect of life that keeps him up half the night."

"Oh? Like what?"

Anna greeted the waitress with a smile and took the menu she handed her. "The other day he proposed the question: What is more important to a person—the heart, soul or mind?"

"I see what you mean. What was your answer?"

"Mind. It controls everything in you."

He laughed. "I'd have thought you would say heart."

"Why?"

"Most women do."

"That's a sexist remark. If your mind tells your heart to stop beating, it does."

He inclined his head, a smile shimmering in his dark eyes. "You're so right, and it was a sexist remark— unintentional, of course. I personally think the soul's the most important part of a person. It's your essence—what makes you different from everyone else."

She flipped open her menu. "David felt the same way. We had a lively little discussion about it."

"He sounds like an interesting man."

"The undergraduates love his classes. He's quite entertaining while educating them."

"That's what I heard about you."

Anna blushed. She hadn't done that in a long while and hated the fact that Ian McGregory could cause her to now. "You checked up on me?"

"Of course. Before I meet with a person, I always like to find out as much as I can."

"No surprises that way," she murmured, disconcerted by the fact that this man had delved into her life. Again she remembered someone's intrusive thoughts trespassing in her mind earlier. Again she dismissed that as a possibility.

"I don't like surprises."

"Not many people do." Anna began to study the menu, the words blurring together. Her thoughts centered on the warning bell ringing in her mind declaring nothing was as it seemed.

When the waitress reappeared to take their order, Anna snapped the still unread menu closed and said, "I'll have the chicken cashew salad and a glass of raspberry tea."

Ian gave his menu to the waitress. "The same."

"You don't seem a salad type of guy."

"I don't know if I should ask. What kind of guy do I seem?"

"Steak and potatoes."

"I have found when eating in an unknown restaurant often the person who's familiar with the place knows what's best on the menu."

"That's logical."

"I'm always logical."

"You don't go on hunches in your job?"

"I didn't think you believed in hunches."

"I didn't say that. I said that female intuition and male hunches are only the product of subtle messages subconsciously received by the person and transmitted to the person's consciousness."

"To answer your question, yes, I have been known to go on a hunch before. But I still rely mainly on the facts."

"In my field I think it's important to rely on facts gathered logically and systematically."

"Then you've never gone with a hunch?" Ian asked, his dark gaze ensnaring hers in a dangerous trap she needed to avoid.

Anna thought back to when she was a child and the pain some of her "hunches" had caused her. "Not in years. If I want my work to be respected in the field, I must back it up with concrete data."

The intensity in his regard sharpened as though he could probe beneath her surface. "Your work is important to you?"

She wanted to look away but found it hard to tear her gaze from his. "Yes. Isn't yours?"

"Very."

That one word, spoken with such quiet fierceness, hung between them as though time came to a standstill for a few seconds. Anna shivered. She realized as she finally shifted her gaze to the waitress approaching the table that she wouldn't want to come between Ian McGregory and whatever was his objective.

The waitress set their salads in front of them along with their glasses of tea and warm fresh bread coated with melted cheese. Usually this was her favorite lunch at Molly's Cafe, but the food held no appeal for Anna today. Too much had happened. While Ian heartily dug into his salad, she picked up her fork, stabbed one piece of lettuce and slowly brought it to her mouth.

"How did you get involved in this case you're working on?"

He took a sip of his tea. "I've always kept track of unexplained deaths. In the past few years I began to see a pattern developing. He moves around, which makes it difficult for the local authorities to become suspicious, to see a connection among the multiple deaths."

"Years?"

"Yes, I've been tracking this killer for over four years."

"And you're sure it's a man?"

"Yes. All the victims are women, and he likes to get

close to them."

"No description of him?"

"I believe he changes his appearance each time. I can't get a description that matches."

"Are you sure there is a case? That there's one killer?"

"Yes—call it a hunch if you must." He put his fork down and leaned across the table. "I need to go through Sandra's things. I want to take a look at her bedroom where she was found. Did she keep a diary? Would she have emailed anyone about this man? Who are her friends? I need your help, Anna."

Three

Ian felt Anna's gaze bore into him as he moved about her sister's bedroom, touching objects that Sandra had touched. Nothing. No sense of what had happened came to him. That was what he'd been afraid of. This room might as well have been a black void to him. He had no sense of who Sandra Stanfield was. He knew a crime had probably been committed in this very room, and there should be a residue of intense emotions left lingering in some object.

He laid his hand on her pillow, and a flicker of fear tingled along his fingertips then vanished. Desperate to retain the feeling, he dug his fingers into the soft material. Nothing. He needed Anna's help, and yet she remained by the door.

Anna hesitated in the doorway. Now that this might be the scene of a crime, she didn't want to go inside. She'd watched as Ian prowled the room, running his hand over the dresser, checking the phone to determine her sister's last caller, brushing his fingertips across the bed where Sandra was found, grasping her pillow where she'd laid her head.

"If there's been a crime, should you be touching everything?"

"The scene has already been compromised." He flicked his hand toward the bed. "It's been made."

"I did that when I came to get some of Sandra's things

for the hospital."

He came to her in the doorway, his gaze that intense darkness that sought to delve beneath her surface. "What did her bedroom look like? The bed?"

"There wasn't any indication of a fight or anything, if that's what you're asking." She wanted to take a step back, to give herself some space, but she held her ground, meeting his penetrating look with directness. She wouldn't allow him to intimidate her.

"Describe the scene to me."

His voice held a quiet authority that demanded obedience. Her first instinct was to resist, but one look around her sister's apartment and she instantly remembered why she was here. If he was right...She shuddered and searched her mind for the right words to say.

"I need to know everything. Some small clue you're not even aware of might be just what I need to help solve these crimes."

"It's just that it was several days ago, and I was distraught when I was trying to get her things together."

He clasped her hand and drew her toward the bed. "Sit down. Take your time. Go back to when you entered the apartment."

She sank down next to him on the bed and closed her eyes. Immediately, panic assailed her. Her chest compressed into a tight fist. Her lungs burned. She inhaled deep breaths, but nothing relieved the constriction about her ribcage. Her heart pounded a mad staccato against her breast. The pulsating roar in her ears drowned out all other sounds. The darkness behind her eyes swirled. The pressure in her chest intensified with each hammering beat of her heart. Her sister's fear drove away lucid thought, pushing Anna toward insanity, toward a black void, gaping, ready to swallow her.

"No!" she shot to her feet, gasping for air, clutching her throat. The shallowness of her inhaled breaths did nothing to alleviate the searing in her lungs.

"What's wrong?" Ian gripped her arms, pressing her back against him.

"I—I—" Words failed her, her mind still awash with her sister's fear.

"Take deep breaths." He rubbed his hands up and down her arms, then as though that wasn't enough, he spun her around to face him. "Breathe."

His image rotated and tilted. She blinked and drew more air into her lungs, trying to fill them. "Sandra—" Again she experienced the black void. Her legs started to give away.

Steadying her, he dragged her against him and wrapped his arms about her, as though willing his strength into her. "Anna, what happened?"

Cold, so cold. She shook against him, clinging to him as if he were her lifeline. Reality shimmered in the distance like a mirage.

"Did you experience something just then?"

The concern in his voice almost made her trust him, a complete stranger. But in the end her old fears took over. "No, Sandra's situation just struck me finally. I don't think until I came in here I fully realized I might not get my sister back," she murmured, unable to tell this man the complete truth. People didn't understand, never had.

"Come on. Let's get out of this room." He assisted her into the living room and sat with her on the couch, his arm still about her.

Slowly, with deep breaths, her heartbeat returned to a steady pace, just a shade faster than normal. The tightness in her chest eased enough that when she breathed, her lungs didn't feel on fire. "I think you're right. Someone tried to kill my sister."

"Why do you say that? What happened in there?"

Oh, God. She didn't want to have to go through this again. She didn't want to see the doubtful look in his eyes. "Sandra and I have always been close..." she searched for a word to describe their connection, "on one level."

"What level?"

"Let's just say I can tell when something isn't right with her." *If I allow myself to open up,* she added silently. Her experience in the bedroom only reinforced every reason she avoided exploring that avenue.

"You did experience something in there. Describe it." His voice was gentle but a command nevertheless. "I know this won't make sense to you, but I could feel my sister's panic, her struggle to free herself." She slanted a look to see his expression and was surprised to see no skepticism in his eyes.

"I thought you said there wasn't any evidence of a fight."

"There wasn't. Her bed was messed up, as if she'd been sleeping in it. There were some articles of clothing on the floor. But my sister is a messy housekeeper. Nothing unusual."

"So you picked up and made the bed?"

"Yes, a habit of mine. I'm not a messy housekeeper."

"Tell me why you think she struggled, then."

Anna glanced at Ian then away. She couldn't look into his eyes at the moment. There was something about his gaze that demanded the truth, that demanded surrender. At times when she peered at him, she felt as though he could push his way into her and become a part of her.

She shook her head. "I can't explain it, really. I just know she fought whatever happened to her." She couldn't keep the frustration from sounding in her voice. All through her childhood she had tried to explain it to people until finally she'd stopped trying and swore she never would again. How do you explain things you know to be true despite logic?

He took her still-trembling hands and held them cupped between his. "I need to know whatever you know. This man must be stopped."

"I know, and I want to help. Let me see if I can remember the day I came to get Sandra's things." Anna closed her eyes and thought back to that time. "It was mid-afternoon. I had been at the hospital all morning with Sandra, hoping she would regain consciousness. I let myself into her apartment. Even though we aren't close, I do have a key."

"What was your first impression when you came inside?"

Anna ran the scene through her mind. Walking up to the apartment. Inserting the key and unlocking the door. Stepping inside. "It was too neat for Sandra. That was my first impression."

"Any thoughts on that?"

"Sandra was trying to impress someone. She rarely cleaned up unless someone special was coming over."

"Okay. Where did you go next?"

"I went to check her answering machine. I wanted to see if there were any messages I'd need to handle. Anyone I needed to let know about Sandra."

"Were there any messages?"

"No. Which seemed a bit odd. She often saves messages for weeks. She hates writing down things. She leaves them on the machine instead until she can get to them. Every time I've been over here there are always several on it. Once she had ten, and I remarked on that. She shrugged and said she erases them when she has to."

He rubbed her hands between his as though willing his warmth into her cold fingers. "What did you do next?"

For a second Anna couldn't think beyond the fact that

his hands surrounded hers, his body heat surging into her through his touch, demanding her surrender.

"Anna?"

She tugged her hands from his grasp. "After that I went into the bedroom. You know, except for the clothes on the floor, it looked neat, too." Anna's eyes flew open. "She was expecting a man, and she was hoping to end up in bed with him. She would never clean up for a girlfriend. She hated housework."

"Contrary to you?"

"Oh, no. I hate housework as much as Sandra, but I do it because I hate a messy house more. When I get rich and famous, I'll hire a maid."

Ian smiled. "I have a maid out of necessity. I'm much like your sister and you, but I don't have your determination to do it anyway."

His smile had a way of reaching into her and easing the tension. Warmth flowed through her. Calmness descended, and the fear she'd felt in the bedroom dimmed to a faint memory.

"Was there anything else you can think of that was strange about the room?"

"Not about the room. But the friend who found Sandra told me she was naked under the sheet. Sandra didn't like to sleep without a nightgown on. Said if she ever had to leave in a hurry in the middle of the night she would be dressed. She had this fear about a fire starting while she was sleeping. So see, her being naked doesn't make sense."

"This all leads me to believe that someone was with her right before she went into a coma. It supports my theory."

"Why didn't I think this was strange at the time?"

"Because you weren't looking at it from the standpoint of being a crime."

"Still, I should—"

"Don't go there, Anna." The command was back in his voice.

"I feel like I've let Sandra down."

"The police wouldn't have done anything. They don't know what I know."

"How about that unexplained death a few months back? What did they say about that?"

"I haven't shared it with them."

"Why not?"

"Because I'm here unofficially."

She scooted away from him and twisted to face him on the couch. "When were you going to tell me that? You led me to believe you were officially working on a case."

"I am, just unofficially."

"But if you have evidence that crimes have been committed, why aren't the authorities looking into it?"

"My evidence is a hunch and a pattern I've found. This killer's very clever."

Anna stared down at her hands that he'd held so tenderly a moment before. The brand of his fingers lingered on her skin. "You nearly had me convinced there was a crime here."

"There was."

Her gaze collided with Ian's. "Why are you so passionate about this case? Do most agents go to the length you are to solve a crime?"

"Some do."

A feeling he was being evasive gnawed at her composure. She wanted things all wrapped up in a neat little package, no surprises. She was sure he was holding back something, and her anger surged to the foreground.

"I don't think you're telling me the truth. At least not the whole truth." She rose and put some distance between them. When she was near him, she felt some of her control slipping, as though he exerted some kind of influence over her.

"What do you want to know about me? About the case?"

"Where do you live?"

"Washington, D. C. when I don't have to travel."

"How long have you been here?"

"Only a day. I took some time off. I feel I'm getting close to the killer this time."

"How long have you been with the FBI?

He pinned her with the intense gaze that could strip away layers of her carefully structured composure. "Eighteen years."

"You don't look a day older than thirty, and unless the FBI takes in children—How old are you?" Surprise and skepticism laced her voice.

"Forty, and thanks for the compliment."

"I'm not sure it was a compliment," Anna grumbled, amazed at how youthful the man looked.

"Well, I will take it as one." His mouth lifted in a lopsided grin meant to melt her resistance.

The smile almost worked—then she remembered Sandra's fear and what could be at stake here. "What do you usually do at the FBI?"

"I oversee a computer division that keeps track of various activities."

"Ah, that pattern you talked about."

"Among other things."

"Why isn't anyone taking you seriously?"

"No concrete evidence to convince them. The FBI likes that. I'm what you would call a computer nerd, not a field agent anymore."

Computer nerd? He didn't look at all like a man who sat in front of a screen all day. His tall build was muscular, not an ounce of fat on him. "Why did you go around touching everything in Sandra's bedroom?"

He peered away for a few seconds then back at her. "After listening to your opinions, you might consider this a bit unorthodox. I get vibes from physical objects."

"The hunches you were talking about?"

"If you want to call them that. When I see and feel things, I get a sense of a person."

"That can be easily explained, Mr. McGregory. People reveal their personalities in what they select to wear, read, eat. You're probably just very good at deducing a person's character from what they own."

"Whatever it is has helped me in my work."

"I can usually find a logical reason why something has happened." She realized she had become quite good at doing that.

"Then how do you explain connecting with your sister on a certain level most people don't?"

She began to prowl the room, much like he had earlier in the bedroom. "Even though Sandra and I aren't close now, at one time we were very close. Inseparable."

"What happened?"

Anna shrugged. "We drifted apart. Different interests."

"But you live in the same town. Work at the same university. Are you sure you drifted apart, as you say?"

"I thought I was the one asking the questions."

"What else do you want to know?"

"How long are you going to be here?"

"That depends."

"On what?"

"On what I discover. What happens with Sandra."

Anna stopped prowling and turned toward him. "What do you mean? Is she in any more danger?"

Ian rose. "I'm not going to kid you, Anna. Yes, Sandra could be in danger. If she comes to, she can identify the man. Give me something to go on. No one else has been able to do that."

"If she comes to? You don't think she will?"

"No one has yet survived whatever it is he's doing to kill these women."

"How can I keep her safe?" Panic that was hers alone surfaced.

"Since it's difficult for you or me to watch her twenty-four hours a day, I would suggest hiring a bodyguard. I know a woman who is very good at watching over people. I can contact her and make the arrangements."

"I don't have much money. Neither does Sandra." This was all moving too fast for her to comprehend totally. Attempted murder. Still in danger. Bodyguard.

"I'll take care of it for you. Terri owes me a big favor."

Even though his tone of voice was reassuring, doubts plagued Anna. "Why are you doing this?" Tension built behind her eyes, pulsating.

"You'll find I don't do anything halfheartedly. I want this killer, and I don't want your sister to be another one of his victims."

"I can pay this woman, but it'll have to be over a period of time, if she'll agree to that."

"I said I would take care of it."

"No. Sandra's my sister." She massaged her temples.

"It's okay to accept help, Anna."

"From family maybe, not a stranger."

"Then have dinner with me and get to know me. That way I won't be a stranger."

There was a part of her that wanted to say yes, but something inside held the words back. "I have plans for this evening."

"Then I'll contact Terri and make the arrangements for her to come here."

"So long as you realize I'll pay for this, given some time." Anna thought about going to the bank and getting a second mortgage on her house. She wouldn't let Sandra down. She would do anything to keep her sister alive. Not being aware of what was going on in Sandra's life, she had a lot to make up for.

"Fine. If that's the way you want it. Terri should be here tomorrow. I'll meet you at the hospital, say, by nine tomorrow morning."

Suddenly Anna needed to get out of her sister's apartment. She felt as if the walls were closing in on her, the air stale, oppressive. The throbbing pain in her head intensified. "I'll be there," she murmured, heading for the door.

***

An antiseptic odor mingled with the sweet scent of roses wilting in a vase in Sandra's hospital room. Anna stared at the flowers on the windowsill. Blood red. An omen of things to come? She quivered and straightened in the chair.

Rolling her head around on her shoulders, she tried to work the kinks out of her neck. She ached in places she hadn't known existed. Sitting up all night in an uncomfortable chair guarding her sister wasn't great on the body.

Anna rose, stretched, then walked to the window and opened the shade. Bright sunlight flooded the room, making a mockery of her dark mood. Looking back at her sister lying helplessly in the hospital bed, she ran her hand through her short hair and wondered how in the world everything had gotten so messed up.

How did she think she could protect her sister? She was one hundred and ten pounds and only five feet three inches. What kind of skills did she think she had to fight off an attacker? And worse, how would she know who the attacker was? Even if there was an attacker?

Again she tunneled her fingers through her hair, trying to bring some kind of order to the mop of curls before Ian

McGregory showed up. Her thoughts felt as jumbled as she knew her hair looked. A night without much sleep wasn't conducive to battling wits with the stranger she'd met yesterday, or conducting her class later that morning. Yet, if she lay down right now in a comfortable bed, she knew she wouldn't sleep. Her mind wouldn't rest. All night she'd fought off visions of an imaginary attacker, of Ian McGregory.

The door swished open, and Dr. Nelson entered the room. Surprise flickered across his features when he saw Anna standing by the window. "Didn't I tell you you needed to rest and not stay here all night? You aren't doing your sister any good if you exhaust yourself and get sick."

Anna waved her hand in the air as though to dismiss his concerns. "I couldn't sleep, so I might as well keep Sandra company." She didn't want to worry Dr. Nelson about her sister's life possibly being in danger.

"Do you want me to give you something so you can sleep better?"

She shook her head, remembering the dreams she'd had the past few nights. A tremor quaked down her spine, and she crossed her arms over her chest, trying to warm her suddenly cold body.

"Then let me buy you a cup of coffee, and you can tell me about some nice places to go eat in Lexington."

"You don't know?"

"I've only been here a few months and haven't had the time to explore the city."

"Perhaps another time. I have to pass right now. I'm waiting for a—" She paused, really not sure how to describe her relationship with Ian McGregory. "—for a friend."

Dr. Nelson gave her a smile that transformed his ordinary features into a pleasing countenance. "Perhaps another time then," he murmured and started to leave.

"Doctor?"

He glanced over his shoulder at her.

"Did you come in here for a reason?"

"Oh, yes," he said with a blush. He walked to the bed and ran a brief check on Sandra, then hurried into the corridor.

Not two minutes later Ian came into the room, a tall woman right behind him. Anna was struck by her beauty. Her long black hair hung in thick waves down her back. Her startlingly blue eyes were mesmerizing, much as Anna felt Ian's were. He and this woman looked different, and yet Anna sensed a strong connection between them. Lovers? That thought disturbed her for some reason. She quickly dismissed it and concentrated on what Ian was saying.

"Anna, this is Terri Carlson, the woman I told you about yesterday. She's agreed to guard your sister while I try to figure out what's going on."

Anna shook Terri's hand and liked the strong feel of her handshake. "As I'm sure Ian has told you, I'll pay for your services. I'm not sure what the threat is to my sister, but I don't want to take any chances with her life."

"She'll be safe with me. I have a friend who will relieve me when I need it. You don't need to worry about your sister."

Anna believed the woman. Terri Carlson had a no-nonsense approach coupled with a warm smile that reassured Anna that Sandra was in good hands. "Well, then I'll leave you to do your job. I have a class in an hour. I'll be visiting later today." She started for the door, not physically up to verbally dueling with Ian.

"Anna, please wait. I have something to ask you."

Ian said a few words to Terri that Anna couldn't hear, then came toward her. She glanced at the tall woman who sat at her sister's side and saw compassion and interest in her gaze. She wondered what Ian had told Terri about the situation, about her.

Outside in the hall he fell into step next to her as they walked toward the elevators. "Was staying with your sister all night the plans you had?"

"First Dr. Nelson and now you. Do I look that bad that you can tell I stayed here last night?"

Ian halted, clasping her hand to stop her progress to the elevator. He peered deep into her eyes. "No, you don't look bad at all. I came by last night myself to watch Sandra and found you."

"I didn't see you."

"I didn't want to disturb you."

Her heartbeat slowed while the feel of his hand about hers sent an awareness through her that sharpened her senses to him. She breathed in his distinctive male scent and wondered if she would ever forget his earthy smell. That thought led her to wonder about how he would taste on her tongue.

Oh, my Lord. She must be more tired than she thought. She had no business thinking that. Maybe she should cancel her morning class, go home to bed and pray sleep would return her sanity.

"After what you told me, I didn't think Sandra should be alone," She finally said, realizing she had been staring at him. A blush tinted her cheeks at remembering what she had been thinking concerning Ian McGregory. "What did you need to talk to me about?"

"Have dinner with me tonight?"

She opened her mouth to say no when he placed his finger over her lips. "I won't accept that you have plans tonight unless they're with me."

Her tongue came out to lick where his finger had touched briefly. "How did you know I was going to say no?" she asked, rather than focusing on the fact that his eyes compelled her to accept. His words, spoken in a soft command, demanded it, too.

"I can read it in your eyes. You're an open book. Will you have dinner with me?"

"Come to my house at seven. I'll fix dinner for us." She couldn't believe she had said that. She rarely had people over. She loved to cook but didn't often do it for others at her place. Her house was her sanctuary where she retreated from the world.

"I'll bring a bottle of wine, then."

As she walked toward the elevator, she felt his gaze on her and was stunned that he was coming to eat dinner with her. She had wanted to say no and had ended up saying yes. How could that be?

Four

Anna wasn't sure why she went to Molly's Cafe after visiting Sandra in the hospital, but she found herself pulling into the parking lot beside the restaurant and walking toward the door. In stark contrast to how she felt inside, the day was beautiful with not a cloud in the sky. Sometimes life went on and left a person behind, Anna thought, entering the cafe.

She spotted David Pierce at a table by himself and headed for it. She needed to be with people she liked and cared about. Sandra's situation was taking its toll on her emotions, not to mention her determination not to experience her childhood trauma all over again.

Anna stopped next to David's table. "Hi, can you use some company?"

He smiled up at her, his light blue eyes twinkling. "If it's you, anytime." He patted the seat next to him. "Sit and tell me what's wrong."

"Am I that obvious?"

"To a trained eye and a friend. Otherwise, you appear as though you have not a care in the world."

"Good. I would hate to think my students thought I was falling apart today while I'm lecturing them on the brain."

"Such an interesting topic. Did they fall asleep?"

Anna chuckled. "If I didn't know you better, I would be offended. I happen to know you're fascinated with how the brain works."

The waitress appeared, and Anna ordered a cup of coffee, strong and black to keep herself alert. If she thought it would help, she would go home and take a long nap before her dinner engagement with Ian. But she knew herself. She would never be able to rest and clear her mind enough to sleep, no matter how exhausted she was from the past few days. Her mind refused to shut down, and if she was totally honest with herself, she wasn't sure she wanted to dream.

"The brain is just one of many body parts that fascinate me." The corners of David's mouth cocked in a self-mocking grin.

"I don't think I should pursue that."

Some of her weariness lifted with David's light repartee. He was just what she needed at the moment. He could always make her feel better. Looking at him, she wondered why she wasn't attracted to him. He was handsome in a rough sort of way, with dark blond hair and light blue eyes that were often full of laughter. But she did sense an intensity behind that laughter that intrigued her. Of course, she shouldn't be surprised there was a depth to the man. After all, he was a professor of philosophy.

David took her hand and leaned across the table. "You know, I've been wondering why we've never gone out on a date. You're certainly an attractive woman, Anna Stanfield."

"Oh, my, be still my heart." She fluttered her hand in front of her face, surprised that he had been thinking the same thing she had. Or, as Ian McGregory had said, was her face like an open book?

"Is it because we're such good friends?"

Anna didn't have an answer for him. She was thankful the waitress chose that moment to place her cup in front of her. David and she had been friends for three years, ever since he had come to the university from New York. When the waitress left, Anna shrugged. "Who knows?"

David looked at her intently. "The mysteries of the heart?"

"Exactly."

"Too complex for me. That's why I'm a confirmed bachelor."

"David. Anna. I'm glad you two are here. It's been a tough day." Another fellow professor, Sloan Reed, pulled out the chair next to Anna and sat.

"I'm afraid to ask what's happened." Anna took a sip of her coffee.

"Government red tape. You have to justify every cent they give you. Then one of my lab rats got loose. You should have seen me chasing him all over the place. I do declare I've gotten my exercise for the week."

Anna laughed at the picture of Sloan running around his lab trying to catch a rat. His perfect good looks and immaculate dress were legendary on campus.

"I think I'm offended by your humor, Anna, my dear." Sloan waved for the waitress to come take his order.

With the addition of Sloan to their table, Anna noticed it wasn't long before several more people came and sat with them. Dr. Sloan Reed was like a magnet drawing an audience wherever he went, especially the women. No wonder his biology classes were always full the first day registration was open. He was relatively new to the campus, but his popularity was becoming legendary.

Anna reclined back in her chair and let the conversation flow around her, absorbing the laughter, the companionship of the group of professors and students. For a brief hour she pushed her worries concerning her younger sister to the back of her mind to deal with later.

Anna, I'm coming for you.

She flinched, her eyes growing round as she scanned the cafe. Beads of sweat broke out on her forehead while despondency blanketed her, causing her to tremble.

"Anna, what's your woman's intuition tell you about that?"

Nonplused, she shook her head, trying to rid herself of the sensation that she had just been invaded. She threw up her barriers to guard her innermost self and concentrated on what Sloan was asking her. "Excuse me?"

"Are you all right?" Sloan's brow creased while his intense gaze fixed on her.

She nodded.

"I wanted to know your take on the latest investigation concerning funding irregularities. Using your woman's intuition, of course."

"Now, Sloan, you know I don't believe in women's intuition, so it would be hard for me to answer that."

"Just the facts, ma'am." Sloan did a great imitation of Joe Friday from *Dragnet*.

"Why, yes, you're so very right, Dr. Reed. That's the only thing that should matter." Anna smiled sweetly at him, then winked.

Sloan roared with laughter. "Oh, my dear, you have indeed led a sheltered life if you think that. It looks like I'm going to have to rescue you."

"But I'm not a damsel in distress," she said, aware that she probably was if what Ian McGregory said was true.

"Yes, you are. You just don't know it." Sloan went down on a knee next to her chair and clasped her hand. "Fair lady, please say you'll go to the faculty party with me Friday night."

Anna blushed, her cheeks hot. "How can I refuse."

He grinned and winked at her. "You've made my day, fair lady."

***

Anna sautéed the onions and garlic, their aroma saturating the kitchen. While they cooked, she went to the refrigerator and withdrew the ground chuck, tomatoes and spices she would use in the spaghetti sauce. This was just what she needed after the past few days. When she was stressed, she enjoyed cooking. She had been known to get up in the middle of the night and bake bread, cookies and cakes because she couldn't sleep. She tried not to do that often because that meant she had to eat them or give them away. Her friends were beginning to groan when they saw her coming with a box of goodies, declaring they would never be able to keep the weight off if she continued her all night baking sessions.

After putting the meat into the skillet, she cut up the fresh tomatoes for the sauce. This would be a quick version of the all day spaghetti she really liked to make. Ian would be here in a while, and she wanted it at least to be simmering when he came.

By the time she had finished preparing the dinner, she felt calmer. Sandra was safe for the time being with Terri guarding her. Tonight Anna was determined to find out what she could from Ian and then demand that he accept her help. Her sister's life was at stake, if he was to be believed. Today she had made a decision. She would be actively involved in finding out who was responsible. She didn't like what was happening to her, and she'd never been the type to sit back and wait for things to happen around her.

As she set the table in the kitchen, the doorbell rang. She hurried to answer it, anticipation at seeing Ian again causing her to check her appearance in the entrance hall mirror. Her cheeks were flushed from the stove's heat, certainly not from excitement at seeing him. Her short auburn hair was a mass of curls about her face, and her large blue eyes appeared tired, dull. She paused at the door, took a deep breath, then opened it.

The sight of Ian on her porch, looking casually handsome in black jeans and a black T-shirt, sent her heart beating a shade faster. Black suited him. He reminded her of the night.

"Come in," she said and stepped to the side.

"Mmm. It smells delicious. I'm definitely a firm believer that a way to a man's heart is through his stomach."

"I won't touch that comment."

He grinned, a slight uplifting of the corners of his mouth that was much too sexy. "For a guy who knows every fast food restaurant near his house, this is a treat. Thank you for inviting me." He held up a bottle of merlot. "This is my donation to the meal. I can handle going to a store and making a purchase."

"You don't cook?" She led the way into the living room.

"I have when I need to. It's just not one of my favorite things."

"What are your favorite things?"

Anna sat on the couch and immediately realized her mistake. After placing the red wine on the coffee table, Ian sank down next to her, too close. His nearness prodded her heart to beat even faster. The power of the man radiated outward, threatening to prevail over her. That thought set an alarm off deep inside her and strengthened her natural wariness.

"I like to read. I play a mean game of tennis. Otherwise, my life is taken up with my work."

"What made you become an FBI agent?" Anna settled back, forcing herself to relax, to be less aware of the man so close that she could reach out and run her hands through his black hair if she wanted—which she didn't. *Liar,* a little voice in her head declared.

"It's simple. I like hunting bad people."

A hunter. That didn't surprise her. If she'd believed in reincarnation, in one of Ian's past lives, he would have been a warrior who fought to protect what was his. Again she couldn't picture him sitting in front of a computer screen all day. "I can't see you with a computer." She voiced her doubts out loud and watched his reaction.

Not one flicker of emotion passed across his face. "My work with computers has been extremely beneficial in a lot of investigations." Humor entered into his eyes. "What do you see me doing?"

"I see you playing a more active role in hunting, as you say, the bad guy."

He pinned her beneath his probing regard. "We use whatever means we are good at. I'm good at finding patterns, and computers help with that."

The tone in his voice proclaimed the subject was closed. Anna's curiosity was aroused.

"Why are you a professor of psychology?" Ian asked after a moment of uncomfortable silence.

"It's simple. I like figuring out people." But she was having a hard time figuring him out. She wanted to be able to put him into a neat little category. She couldn't. Too many facets.

"There are times I use your type of expertise."

"I'm glad you feel that way because I have a favor to ask of you."

He stared at her, the intensity back in his eyes, his natural wariness erected. "What?"

"I want to help you with this case."

He swore beneath his breath. "Why did I know you were going to say that."

"A hunch?"

"Anna, this isn't a game. This is deadly serious."

She trembled. "I know it is. This is my sister we're talking about. Besides, I might be able to help you. I do know people, and I also know a lot of Sandra's friends. If I don't help you, I'll just do it on my own. I have to do something."

"Do you always resort to blackmail?"

"If it will get what I want, yes." She gave him a smile she hoped would charm him.

"You know this man could be anyone. You can't trust anyone."

"Even you?"

"If you're as smart as I think you are, yes. Beware of everyone, including me."

Another tremor shook her body. "If I wasn't scared before, I am now."

"Good. You need to be. I'd never forgive myself if anything happened to you."

"Why should it? I can't believe the man would have anything to do with me. I'm too close to Sandra. That would expose him faster than anything." For a few seconds she thought about that silent message she had felt earlier in the cafe. Again a chill ran through her body, making her hug her arms to herself.

Ian stared at her for a long moment. Intensity pulsated from him. "This man is capable of anything. He may be getting cocky. He's been doing this for years and not getting caught."

"Then that means he'll make a mistake, and you'll get him."

"Oh, Anna, I wish it were that simple."

She tilted her head to the side. "I'm getting the feeling you aren't telling me everything. If I'm going to be your partner in this, I need to know what you know, or I could be in more danger."

"I haven't agreed to you being my partner."

"The blackmail didn't work?"

He glanced away, his brow furrowed. "This goes against my better judgment, but I guess we could try working together for a while. No promises, however."

"Thanks, Ian. I knew you would see it my way."

Anna impulsively threw her arms around his neck and kissed his cheek. Now *that* was a big mistake! she decided one second later. He captured her face between his hands and stared intently into her eyes. His dark depths drew her in. She felt as though he were probing her mind, reaching deep into her. Startled, she pulled away, severing the connection.

She rose, needing to put some space between them. "Let me get us some wine glasses, then you can open the bottle." She hurried from the room, feeling as if the imprint of his hands were still branded into her cheeks and not sure how to combat these feelings flowing through her.

She searched her cabinets for her wine glasses, flustered by her reaction to his touch. When she found what she was looking for, she took them down, noticing that her hands trembled. She retrieved the corkscrew from the drawer, determined to be composed when she went back into the living room. She couldn't allow Ian to sidetrack her, even though there was an aura about him that fascinated her—frightened her. She didn't understand these mixed feelings and hoped it was because she was so tired. She was determined to get a good night's sleep later. Then everything would look better tomorrow, even her situation with Sandra. She wished she would wake up and find that this was all a dream, that Sandra was at the library, buried in her books. But that wasn't going to happen, she realized. Her sister's life might depend on her ability to collaborate effectively with Ian.

When she rejoined him in the living room, she placed the glasses on the table and watched as he opened the bottle then poured the wine. His movements were precise and economical, something she was beginning to realize summed up the man. He would be a part of her life until this mystery surrounding her sister was solved, and somehow she would make sure they worked together, even if she didn't totally trust him.

He handed her a glass, then lifted his. "To a successful partnership."

The word, partnership, brought to mind something entirely different than what she was sure he'd meant. She pictured them working as a team, too close to be considered professional. A blush tinted her cheeks, and she averted her face, hoping he didn't see the added color. She suspected he would know what she was thinking, especially if he looked into her eyes.

"So what aren't you telling me, Ian?" she asked, putting her glass down.

"I have nothing concrete to tell you. If I did have something concrete, the FBI would be involved."

"Again we're back to those hunches of yours."

His sharp gaze snared hers. "What are you afraid of, Anna?"

Her throat constricted. "That my sister will die." Which was the truth, but not the whole truth. She was also afraid to re-experience the pain of her childhood, but she couldn't let Ian know that. "I should have been there for her. I should have realized something was going on."

"And how were you suppose to realize that? Are you clairvoyant?"

"No," she answered immediately, astonished at how close he was to the truth. "But what if she doesn't come out of the coma? I have so many things I want to say to her. If I had bothered to talk to Sandra more and demanded to know what was going on in her life, maybe this man wouldn't have gotten to her."

"You're too hard on yourself. Regrets won't change anything."

"Do you have any sisters or brothers?"

He brought his glass to his lips and took a long sip, his gaze connected to hers over the rim. "No. I had a sister. She died years ago."

"Oh, I'm sorry." She reached out and touched his hand. "I shouldn't have said anything, but I wanted you to realize how important this is to me."

"I do, Anna. I do." He grasped her hand and held it. "Terri won't let anything happen to Sandra." He sent her a grin that left his eyes cold. "His luck will change, and I'll be there to get him."

"So tell me everything you think you know about this man. Maybe something you tell me might strike me as familiar."

"I doubt anything I know will help you. I found he changes with every woman."

"Like a chameleon?"

Ian blinked, surprise evident in his expression for a second before he shuttered his look. "Yes, like a chameleon. Which makes it very difficult to catch him."

"What kind of woman is he attracted to?"

"Now, that's where I've had some success, because all the women have similar traits."

"Well, knowing Sandra, that means shy, sheltered women."

"And beautiful. They are all striking in appearance. Tall, blond haired and blue eyed."

"Well, that leaves me out. I may have blue eyes, but I'm not blond, and I'm certainly not tall," Anna said with a shaky laugh.

"Don't ever think you're safe. He changes his appearance. He can change the profile of his victims just as easily."

The vehement tone of his voice underscored the danger she could be in if she pursued this killer. She wasn't a risk taker, but she knew she couldn't walk away from helping Ian. She had turned away from Sandra when her little sister had demanded Anna come to terms with her "talent."

Anna folded her arms over her chest. "You don't know for sure there's a killer. As you said, you have no concrete proof, or the FBI would be working on this case officially."

"I *know* there's a killer."

"Again we're back to that hunch of yours. You know how I feel about hunches."

"Then how do you account for your—let's say experience, in your sister's apartment?"

A sudden blast of cold chilled her. "My overactive imagination? You had me worked up." She heard the lie in her voice and winced inwardly. She couldn't account for her experience. She didn't want to account for it. She would love more than anything to pull a blanket over her head and hide from the truth. She knew she wouldn't be able to for long. That frightened her more than the thought of a killer out there somewhere stalking another victim.

She started to reach for her glass of wine. Instead, Ian took her hand again and held it between them, a physical link that vibrated to her core.

"Anna, when are you going to stop denying your ability?"

Sweat beaded her upper lip. She knew he felt her damp palm. "My ability?"

"I sense a level of perception in you that goes beyond the ordinary."

She yanked her hand from his grasp and bolted to her feet. "No! I am as normal as the next person."

He shook his head, a sadness in his eyes. "Are you?"

Tension straightened her spine, held her immobile and poised over him on the couch. She fought an age old battle within herself and finally did what she had learned was the only effective way to deal with her situation. She fled. Hurrying from the room, she murmured something about checking on dinner. She couldn't get into the kitchen fast enough. At the stove she paused, tried to draw deep breaths into her burning lungs, and could only gasp. The room tilted, her thoughts spinning out of control. She didn't want this after fifteen years.

Leaning into the counter, she closed her eyes and tried to right her world, to bring order to the chaos. She didn't know he was there until he laid his hand on her shoulder. She sucked in a swallow of air that wasn't nearly enough.

"Please tell me what you're afraid of."

The gentle tone in his voice nearly undid her. The edges of her composure began to unravel. She kept her eyes closed for a few more seconds, then faced him. He stood only a foot away, his presence dominating her space. She had nowhere to go, trapped between the counter and him. She should be alarmed by that fact, but strangely his calmness eased the tension within her, as if he were capable of healing all her past pain.

"As I said earlier, I'm afraid my sister might die before I can make amends for the past few years." She couldn't voice the deeper, more troubling fear. That required trust she didn't know if she would ever have with another human being again.

"I'll do everything I can to protect her. I want her to wake up, too."

"I know Terri is competent, but will she be able to protect Sandra if the man comes after her to finish the deed? My sister is the only one who can identify him." *Will someone be able to protect me if he comes after me?* Anna thought, remembering the warning at the cafe. *Will I be strong enough to fight this killer off?*

"I trust Terri with my life."

The depth of trust revealed in his voice produced a seed of jealousy in Anna. *Are you two lovers?* she wanted to ask and bit the inside of her cheek to keep from saying anything. It was none of her business.

He looked deep in her eyes, connecting with her on a level that should have scared her. "I'm a patient man, Anna. I can wait until you're ready to tell me what's really troubling you. If we're going to work together, we'll have to learn to trust each other."

She opened her mouth to deny what he'd said but clamped it closed before uttering a word. It felt as though he could read her thoughts which she knew was ridiculous. But she didn't want to compound her situation by lying to him.

"Trust? I thought you told me not to trust anyone. Even you."

"You shouldn't. But then you want to be my partner, and I don't relish the idea of fighting you every inch of the way."

"So if I back off and let you do your job without me, I can distrust you all I want?"

He chuckled. "Yes."

She glanced away for a moment, then back at him, the corners of her mouth lifting slightly. "If you'll get the wine, dinner is ready, and we can eat. I'm starved."

When he left to retrieve the wine, Anna sagged back against the counter, glad that it was there to keep her from slipping to the floor. If she didn't know better, she would have sworn Ian had delved deep into her mind and probed her secret places. She shuddered at the thought.

The sound of him returning prompted her to move to the stove and stir the sauce. She inhaled the pot's aroma. "Mmm. Just as I suspected. Ready to be devoured." The forced lightness in her voice caused her words to tumble out quickly. She wasn't a very good actress and wished she had taken drama in school to improve her inadequate abilities. She was never going to be able to fool this man.

"And I'll do my share of devouring."

Anna peered over her shoulder at Ian. The huskiness in his voice weakened her knees. A vision popped into her head that had nothing to do with eating dinner. She saw them on a bed, mouths, hands, bodies hungry for each other. She shook the image from her thoughts, praying that the heat she felt wasn't visible on her cheeks.

***

Terri rose and stretched her aching muscles. When she rolled her head in a slow circle, her long black hair fell forward. She flipped it behind her shoulders and stared at Sandra Stanfield lying in the hospital bed, beautiful, pale—helpless.

She walked over to the young woman and placed her hands on her head. Only a flicker of life pulsed beneath Terri's fingertips, so faint it was barely discernible. It would be easy to snatch the rest of Sandra's energy from her. She was so vulnerable.

But Ian thought Sandra might pull out of the coma, that the woman might be able to help him. Terri didn't think so, but they had to try. The woman was their best lead to date.

The door swished open, and she whirled about, surprised to be caught off guard. That rarely happened. A group of four people entered the room. She relaxed her rigid stance but didn't ease her vigilance. Too many people came in and out of this room. Not ten minutes before the nurse had visited, and right before that Dr. Nelson.

"I thought Anna would be here. We came to offer her some company," a handsome looking man said. He stepped forward and offered his hand. "I'm Sloan Reed, a friend of Anna's." He looked her up and down with interest and a question in his gaze.

Terri smiled inwardly but kept a professional demeanor outwardly. "I'm Terri Carlson, a friend of the family." She quickly shook the man's hand.

"Where's Anna?" another man asked behind Sloan.

Sloan glanced back at him. "Now, David, I'm sure this young woman has better things to do with her time than keep tabs on our Anna."

"She said something about going home to prepare dinner for a friend," Terri said, feeling evaluated and categorized.

Sloan appeared stunned. "For a friend? Male or female?"

"Male, I believe, but then I don't keep tabs on Anna."

David laughed. "I think you might have competition, old man."

"How's Sandra doing?" a woman with a bold silver streak through her dark hair asked.

"Nothing's changed. She's still in a coma. Whom should I tell Anna visited?"

"Well, as you know, I'm Sloan Reed, and this cheeky man is David Pierce. And this is Madge Reynolds, our resident do-gooder." Sloan gestured toward the woman with the silver streak. "Last, but not least, is Kayla Masters in the back. Just tell Anna we were at the cafe and decided to pop on over before going our separate ways for the evening."

When the party shuffled out of the room, Terri followed and stood by the door for a long moment, listening to make sure they were really leaving. Groups of people didn't concern her because the killer wouldn't do anything while others were around, but still she couldn't allow herself to slip so deeply into thought that she didn't hear someone approaching.

She cocked her head to the side and continued to listen to the sounds in the hallway. People passed the room. Someone hailed a doctor. She heard the elevator open, and a conversation taking place at the nurses' station.

Then the sound of heavy footsteps coming toward the room, stopping outside the door, alerted her. She moved toward the bed, in between Sandra and whoever might enter the room. A tall, muscular man came inside and stopped when he saw Terri, a furrow on his brow.

"Who are you?" he asked, his deep voice clipped, cold.

"Who are you?" Terri balanced herself lightly on the balls of her feet, ready to spring forward if need be.

"I'm a friend of Sandra's. I work at the library with her. I've been worried about her." He paused, waiting for Terri to say something.

"I'm a friend of the family. Anna had something to do, so I told her I'd sit with Sandra."

"Well, I can take over now. When will Sandra's sister be back?"

"I'm not sure."

As the tall man approached the bed, Terri positioned herself so she could defend Sandra if he made a move toward her. The sharp edginess in his eyes worried Terri.

He took Sandra's hand, then lifted his head to stare at Terri with a narrowed gaze. "Do you mind? I would like a few minutes alone with my friend."

"Yes, I mind. I told Anna I wouldn't leave until she came back." Terri drew herself up straight, her gaze piercing in her appraisal of the young man.

His regard drilled into Terri while his jaw clenched. When he turned back to Sandra, he leaned close to her ear and whispered something so quietly that most people wouldn't have heard. Terri had, however. The man straightened, placed Sandra's hand carefully, some would say lovingly, back at her side and strolled from the room.

Terri was half tempted to go after him, not sure of his intent. But her first priority was Sandra's safety. Still, what had the young man meant when he'd told her he was sorry for their fight?

***

I can't get to her! They have her guarded. Impotent rage slammed through him. He should leave Lexington. He'd played too long here. But thoughts of the power Anna held within her was too much for him to turn away from. He would get to Sandra, and he would have Anna. And then he'd have his sweet revenge on the Hawk.

Five

Anna glanced at the French doors leading out to the terrace, then back at the room full of people—all trying to talk at the same time, all trying to impress the person beside them. Usually these faculty parties didn't bother her, but she realized she shouldn't have come. The darkness beyond the French doors beckoned her.

She opened one and slipped outside, welcoming the cool caress of the spring air, the sweet hint of nature's nectar peppering the breeze. Quickly covering the short distance to the stone wall, she closed her eyes and inhaled deeply.

You can't run from me. I'm always nearby, waiting.

The words assailed her. Her eyes snapped open and scanned the terrace. The very darkness that moments before had called to her suddenly took on sinister depths. The lights from the house spilled across the terrace, drawing her toward their warmth and security. Stubbornly she remained in the shadow, her eyes becoming pinpoints as she searched the blackness.

Angry at the fear that blanketed her, she stiffened her spine and balled her hands at her side. "Why don't you come and get me? Why hide in the shadows? Afraid to face me?"

Silence answered her questions. She flexed her fingers, then curled them into fists, her nails digging into her palms.

Someone opened the French doors and stepped

outside. Anna moved deeper into the darkness, intending to remain hidden, until she heard her name.

"Anna?" Sloan called her again.

"I'm over here." She moved forward to the light's edge.

He walked toward her. "I thought I saw you come out here. Are you all right?"

"This wasn't a good idea. I don't feel like partying while Sandra lies in the hospital."

Sloan clasped her hand and rubbed it between his. "You're cold. Do you want me to take you home?"

"I can call a cab. I don't want you to miss the party because of me."

He laughed. "I don't think I'm going to miss much. Everyone is trying to outdo the next person with his brilliance. Such a waste of time when we all know I am the most brilliant professor in the room."

A smile came to her lips. "I can always count on you to cheer me up."

"Just doing my duty as your date for the evening. Come on. Let's go say good-bye to Dean Collington and his wife. We'll let them think we're two lovebirds sneaking away early for clandestine purposes."

Her own laugh escaped to blend with the noise from the party. "If I hang out with you much longer, I'm not going to have a reputation left. We all know what a womanizer you are."

"You wound me, my dear Anna. I can't help it if I like women. They're much more interesting than my gender."

"I'm not going to argue with you on that."

Sloan took her hand and tugged her toward the French doors. Inside the room the stale air accosted her. She immediately felt the press of people all around her and quickly followed Sloan through the crowd to where Dean Collington stood.

You won't escape me, pretty Anna.

She froze, yanking her hand free of Sloan's. She whirled about. *Where are you?* Faces loomed before her. Voices bombarded her. The room tilted and spun. Swaying on her feet, she blinked several times to clear the haze from her eyes.

"Anna, what's wrong?"

She heard Sloan's concerned voice from afar. Sweat drenched her and rolled down her face, stinging her eyes. An arm came about her to support her against a hard body.

"Move out of the way," Sloan shouted, and the crowd parted.

She brought her hand up to her forehead to wipe the sweat away. More voices of concern reverberated in her mind, but nothing could obliterate the laughing taunt echoing in her thoughts.

Sloan led her to a couch and pushed her gently down upon it. She leaned her head back on the cushion and drew in deep, calming breaths, upset at this open display of weakness. But worry and exhaustion were taking their toll, hammering against her forehead. She had to get herself together quickly so she could leave.

"Anna?" This time it was David calling her name.

She peered at him hovering over her on one side with Sloan on the other. She offered them both a smile that instantly vanished. Beyond the two men were a room full of people staring at her.

"Let me through." Dr. Nelson pushed his way through the crowd and stood between Sloan and David. He lifted her hand and checked her pulse, worry etched into his solemn face.

When he looked at her, the censure in his gaze was evident. "You aren't taking care of yourself, Anna. You're going to end up in a bed right next to your sister."

Dr. Nelson still held her hand in his. His warm grasp

left her feeling even colder. She straightened on the couch, intending to stand up, but he placed his hands on her shoulders and stopped her from rising. "Take it slow and easy, Anna."

She nodded and allowed him to help her to her feet, his touch sending an icy current through her body. She sensed so much death that she couldn't keep her heart from racing. It thundered in her ears and pounded against her chest. With a supreme effort she kept herself upright, even though the urge to sway against him was strong. And in the background she could continue to hear the faint taunt.

A resolve born of desperation took hold. She lifted her chin and scanned the crowd of people surrounding her. Determination pushed the fear away as she looked each one in the eye and silently dared the person to come forward. Not a flicker of recognition crossed anyone's face. The momentary challenge sapped what energy she had left. She grabbed Sloan's offered arm and clung to him as they made their way to the front door.

The hush in the room dissolved instantly when Sloan opened the door and they stepped out onto the porch. A blush heated her cheeks as she thought about being the topic of conversation for the next fifteen minutes. She never liked to call attention to herself.

"I'm sorry you have to leave so early," she murmured as Sloan held the car door open for her and assisted her inside.

He leaned down, close to her face. "It was getting to be boring. You know the only reason you and I go is duty."

Anna watched him stride around the front of his red Corvette and slide in behind the steering wheel. "A necessary evil?"

"Evil. What a delicious word." He slanted a look toward her. "What do you consider evil in this world?"

"The usual things—murder, rape." She massaged her temple, trying to ease the throbbing pain behind her eyes. "Attempted murder," she added, thinking about her sister. "What happened in there?" Sloan threw his sports car into reverse and backed out of the parking space.

Something truly evil, Anna thought and knew she could never voice that out loud. "Not enough sleep this past week."

"How is Sandra doing? Any progress?"

Anna shook her head, then realized that Sloan couldn't see her answer. "No, she's the same as the first day, which I suppose is better than getting worse."

"Do the doctors have any idea what happened to her?"

"Not a clue. Very mysterious." She started to tell Sloan Ian McGregory's theory but stopped herself. For all she knew Sloan could be the man Sandra had been with. He was relatively new to Lexington and loved pretty women. Sandra was shy but beautiful, someone who could turn a man's head. Of course, that could describe thousands of men in Lexington. Ian was right, she couldn't trust anyone.

Sloan pulled into her driveway and hopped out of the car. Rounding the front, he opened her door and helped her out. "I'm sorry this evening turned out so badly." He brought her up against him, combing his fingers through her hair, a smile curving his full lips. "I have time for a cup of coffee."

She started to invite him in, but something warned her not to. "I'm exhausted. Some other time?"

His smile faltered. "Sure. I'm gonna hold you to it, Dr. Stanfield." He settled his arm on her shoulders and began walking her toward the porch.

The light was on, and she didn't remember turning it on. She frowned and tried to think back to when Sloan had picked her up. It hadn't been dark at the time, and she couldn't recall flipping the switch as she left the house.

Tension whipped down her length. She started to tell him she had reconsidered having coffee, then decided her mind was playing tricks on her. She always turned the light on. It had become so automatic that she surely had forgotten doing it. She shrugged the tension away and turned to say good night to Sloan.

He captured her, his arms winding about her and pulling her to him. Before she realized it, he kissed her, his tongue pushing its way into her mouth. She couldn't find any energy to respond. She wasn't upset by the kiss, but it did nothing for her. When Sloan leaned back, staring into her eyes, she could tell her unresponsive reaction had irritated him. He immediately masked his feeling behind a bland expression.

"Good night, Anna." He strode away, leaving her on the porch.

She fumbled for her key and opened her front door. Stepping inside, she collapsed back and drew in calming breaths. She closed her eyes and tried to will strength back into her limbs to make it up the stairs and to her bed.

"Did you enjoy this evening?"

The question came from a pool of darkness in the entrance to the living room. Anna gasped and clasped the door handle, intending to escape. Then Ian moved out of the shadow into the hall light. Impotent rage shook her. She went rigid.

"How did you get into my house?"

"With this." He held up the key she hid out back under a stone in her rock garden.

"How did you find that?"

"A hunch."

"Don't mock me. I'm not in the mood." She shoved away from the door and stormed past him, switching on lights as she made her way.

Brightness flooded the living room, chasing away all

the shadows. She felt better when she swung around to face him. "You weren't invited. Go away before I call your employer and tell him what you're doing."

He moved quickly, so swiftly the action took Anna by surprise. "I came to talk to you about the case and got worried when you weren't here," he said not two feet from her.

"I do have a life that doesn't include you."

"Who was that?"

"None of your business."

"Everything about you is my business."

The predatory tone to his voice nonplused her. She took a step back and hit the couch. "Leave me alone."

In two strides he closed the space between them, trapping her between him and the couch. "I can't do that. You wanted to help, and frankly, I need your help with this case. No one else is—as connected to your sister as you. Now who was that man?"

She balled her hand and would have struck him if he hadn't captured her fist and held it between them. "My life is not up for discussion."

"Where it concerns Sandra it is. You weren't seeing anyone, so why all of a sudden are you going out? What's going on?"

"How do you know I wasn't dating someone?"

"I checked you out—thoroughly."

Stunned, she sat on the couch which she instantly decided was a mistake when Ian eased down next to her. "I'm not a suspect."

"When I work with someone, I find out everything I can about that person. No surprises."

"Everything?" she murmured, wondering if he knew the secret she had worked hard to hide from others.

He nailed her beneath a penetratingly intense look. "Yes, everything, Anna. I know about your abilities."

She started to rise, but he blocked her escape.

"I know you have certain talents that could be useful to me in my investigation. And since we're going to be partners—"

"You're crazy. I don't know what you mean by talents." She plastered herself against the back cushion as far from him as possible, which wasn't far enough.

He chuckled. "Some have accused me of being crazy. But I do get results when I'm determined, and I am determined to get this killer."

Shudder after shudder rippled through her at the very coldness of his words. "Dr. Sloan Reed."

"He was your date?"

She nodded.

"Why?"

The question surprised Anna. "Why not? I had a faculty party to go to, and I don't like attending alone. I may not date much, but I do have friends." She hoped the haughty edge to her voice would discourage further discussion of her dating life, which was nonexistent.

"Next time take me. I don't like you putting yourself in jeopardy until I catch this killer."

"I've known Sloan for—months."

"Exactly. Not long enough."

"Longer than I've known you."

"True. But I'm the good guy, Anna."

"How do I know that for sure?"

"You don't. You'll just have to trust me."

"But you told me not to trust anyone."

"Then listen to your inner voice, the one that used to get you into trouble when you were growing up."

Scenes from her childhood taunted her. "You know about that."

"I told you, I know everything."

"Then you know I don't listen to that voice anymore."

She shoved at him so she could stand, her anger building. He was opening an old wound best left covered.

He reluctantly let her get up. "You should. It's part of you."

She whirled about. "No, it isn't!"

"You may be the only one who can help your sister. I need you to use your talent—not go out with men you think your sister might have been involved with. Too dangerous."

Anna began to shake. She clasped her hands in front of her to still the quivering, but it quickly spread throughout her body. "I have no *talent*. And I'm not investigating on my own."

He was off the couch and in front of her so quickly she blinked several times. He grabbed her arms. "You have a great talent. When you were growing up, people didn't understand it."

"That so-called talent got a boy killed." She wrenched free and scrambled away from him, holding her hand out to stop him from coming toward her. "I want you to leave. Now."

"What's gonna happen when the killer comes after your sister again? Are you going to continue to hide behind your denial?"

The questions were spoken low, with an icy thread running through them that froze Anna. She remembered the voice inside her head at the faculty party. Plowing her fingers through her hair, she sank down onto the floor, curling her legs up against her chest and clasping them.

"You don't understand. It nearly killed me when Kenny died. I can't go through that again."

"Not even for your sister?" He knelt next to her and grasped her shoulder, kneading her taut muscles.

She leaned into his touch, seeking the comfort it offered. Again memories of a childhood best left in the past began to seep into her mind, scenes of humiliation and ridicule parading through her thoughts in Technicolor. *Freak. What am I thinking now?* The taunt replayed itself over and over as though Kenny were standing in front of her and yelling at her—right before she told him what he was thinking and, frightened, he fled across the street, running right into a speeding car.

Anna buried her face in her hands, trying not to see in her mind's eye Kenny lying on the pavement, blood everywhere, staring up at her through unseeing eyes. She shouldn't have let him bait her. From that day forward she swore to herself she would never use her "talent" again. And she hadn't—until she sat on her sister's bed and felt Sandra's ordeal.

"I can't. Isn't there another way?" Her throat closed around the words, tight, aching. "That isn't what I meant when I asked to help you."

"But it is what I meant. What are you afraid of, Anna?"

She lifted her head and looked toward Ian through a blur of tears. "Myself. I couldn't control it. Didn't know what to do with it."

"Tell me about what you call *it.*" He pulled her back against him and cradled her.

She shook her head, not sure she could form the words to explain what she'd gone through. She'd been called a freak so many times that she had begun to feel that way about herself.

"Help me to understand."

The caress of his words soothed her troubled soul, much as his touch did. She wanted to resist, to keep that part of herself locked up deep inside, but she couldn't. She searched for the right words to explain.

He settled his hands on her head, massaging her scalp. Her eyes slid closed under the delicious sensations he generated with his fingertips. She felt seduced into relaxation, her body going limp against his hard one.

"I have a touch of psychic ability, Anna. Maybe I can help you."

His words resonated through her thoughts. His fingers, buried in her hair, continued to rub her head, slowly, hypnotically. "I'm—I'm so tired. I'm scared to sleep."

"Why, Anna?"

Her head fell back against his shoulder. His hands slipped down her neck to the tight cord at the top of her spine. His fingers began their magic there, loosening the taut muscles.

"I don't like my dreams."

"What are your dreams?"

She started to tell him about the night her sister went into a coma, but somewhere in the deep recesses of her mind where she had learned to protect herself at all costs, a warning flashed. She blinked, trying to pull herself up out of the lethargic depths, to guard herself.

"Anna, something will give if you don't relax. I'm worried about you."

Genuine concern enticed her back toward the listlessness.

"That's it. Relax. Let yourself go. Forget everything. We can talk later." His hands kneaded the flesh between her shoulder blades.

Darkness called to her. Her eyelids grew heavier and heavier, and his voice, murmuring soft words that made no sense, sounded farther away with each minute his fingers worked her stiff muscles loose.

Ian knew the second she totally slipped into the realm of sleep. She released the tight hold on her thoughts and surrendered finally. She was a tough one to help. She resisted every attempt, and even in her relaxed state had her guard up. Powerful psychic talent lay beneath a shield she'd erected around herself. He needed to get through to that inner person.

Framing her head again between his hands, he closed his eyes and pushed his way into her mind. Even now she fought him on a subconscious level. He had to be careful. He wanted no trace of himself left in her mind. Quickly, he forged a little deeper, fusing his energy with hers until he felt a small part of her. Only a few minutes—any longer and he put himself at risk of discovery. He backed out reluctantly, wishing he could go farther. Her lure appealed to him more than he cared to acknowledge.

Releasing her head, he cradled her in his arms and lifted her up. With ease he carried her up the stairs to her bedroom and placed her on the green and gold coverlet. After removing her shoes, he found a blanket on top of the chest at the end of the bed and laid it over her, then retreated from the room before he climbed into bed with her.

In the darkened hallway he saw his way easily down the stairs. He thought about leaving and coming back the next morning, but quickly dismissed that. She was his link to the killer—she and her sister. Terri was watching the sister; he would watch her as much as she would let him.

A smile pulled at the corners of his mouth with that thought. She would fight him every inch of the way. She didn't have relationships, but if that was what it took to get close to her and protect her, then so be it.

***

Sunlight poured into the room through the open curtains. Anna could feel it on her face, but all she wanted to do was snuggle down into the covers and surrender to the dark void again. Slowly, though, sensations penetrated her sleep-muddled mind. The delicious aroma of coffee brewing teased her senses. She shifted and realized that she still wore her black dress and even her pantyhose from the evening before. With that realization she shot up in bed, the previous night's events bombarding her with vivid imagery, all centered around Ian McGregory comforting her.

Shock held her immobile as her gaze fastened onto the easy chair by the window. He'd slept there only a few feet from her. She knew it. She could still feel his energy in the room as though it were a palpable force. How had she slept so soundly and not known he was with her? Her control was slipping. She couldn't let that happen, or the past would repeat itself.

Quivering, she squeezed her eyes shut and tried to pull herself together enough to face Ian. Before she lost her nerve, she discarded her torn pantyhose and slid her feet into a pair of slippers. Glancing down at her wrinkled black dress, she shrugged away the concern that she didn't present a very together picture. She needed the man out of her house.

Downstairs she paused in the kitchen doorway, her gaze taking in Ian sitting at her breakfast table, his dark hair tousled, his suit crumpled, and a vulnerability radiating from him that suddenly melted her resolve to be rid of him.

He looked up and trapped her in that intense, penetrating regard of his. Then slowly the corners of his mouth tilted upward, and a light shone from the dark depths of his eyes.

"Good morning, Anna."

The gentle way he said her name totally dissolved any embarrassment she might have at his being in her kitchen so early in the morning, at his sharing the same bedroom and her being oblivious to it. "Do I smell coffee?"

"I made a pot. One of the few things I'm really capable of doing in the kitchen."

She shuffled over to the counter and poured a large yellow mug full of the hot brew, taking in its rich aroma as she lifted it to her mouth and sipped cautiously. She sat across from Ian, concentrating on drinking her coffee while she tried to bring some order to her thoughts. He was much too sexy first thing in the morning, and like any red-blooded American woman she appreciated an attractive man.

"About last night, Anna. Under the circumstances, I didn't want to leave you alone."

His statement forced her to look at him. "What circumstances?"

"I was worried about you."

The warmth in his eyes reached out to her. She felt an inexplicable connection to him. Something had changed between them since the night before. But when she thought back on the evening, so much of it was a blur. She remembered the pain from the past, the concern in his voice, his touch, then—nothing.

"I want to help you, Anna."

"How?"

"By teaching you about your psychic abilities."

She bolted to her feet, knocking her chair over. "No! Never!"

Six

"Is denying what you are working?" Ian placed his mug on the oak table.

"Who are you?" Anna asked, taking a step back, suddenly not sure of anything, least of all the man before her.

"Ian McGregory."

"Quit being flippant. You know what I mean. FBI agents don't go around encouraging psychic abilities in people."

"What about the X-Files?"

"Fiction, and you know it."

He pushed himself to his feet and came around to right her chair. "Sit down, Anna. It's hard to carry on a conversation with you hovering."

She opened her mouth to protest his high-handedness, but he'd already turned his back on her and was pouring himself another cup of coffee, his movements as controlled as the man. She took her seat again.

When he swung back around, his gaze was perceptively sharp. He took the chair across from her. Even with the table between them, he was much too close for her to think rationally. When he got that look in his eyes, the sensations of being assessed and cataloged washed over her.

"I think we need to finish our conversation from last night. What happened to you as a young girl was tragic. It doesn't have to be that way."

She narrowed her eyes. "You have no idea what I went through."

He captured her hand and held it tight. "As I told you in your sister's apartment, I get vibes from objects sometimes. But instead of pushing those feelings away, I embrace them, let them work for me."

She yanked her hand from his. She didn't want the physical connection, didn't want him getting any kind of vibes from her. "And you think that qualifies you to help me through my—problem? You're crazy. Does the FBI know about your talent?"

"I don't broadcast it." The steel tone to his voice vibrated between them, sending out a warning.

"In other words, you've kept it a secret. You're no different than me."

"I manage my talent, not deny it."

"So that makes you better than me?"

"More content, I suspect."

"I'm fine with my life as it is. You're the one who's telling me I'm not."

"When I touched you last night, I sensed a deep sadness within you."

The idea he was getting vibes from her unnerved her. "Of course. My sister is lying in a coma and may not recover. It doesn't take a brain surgeon to figure out that I would be sad." She squeezed her hands together in her lap, keeping them out of his reach.

He shook his head. "No, this is much deeper than that."

"What do you mean?"

"You're at war with yourself."

"I settled that battle long ago."

"Did you? You use a lot of energy denying your innermost self."

She stood again, this time slowly, scooting her chair

back to keep it upright. Exhibiting control was important. "This conversation is at an end. I think you'd better leave now."

"Very well. But I want you to go back to your sister's apartment with me this afternoon."

Her stomach knotted with tension. "Why? We've already gone through it."

"You insisted you wanted to help me. I need you to go back to her apartment and this time truly open yourself up to the psychic energy there."

The knot twisted tighter. "I can't. Why don't you go and use your abilities?"

"Because you're tied to your sister emotionally. I'm not, and the emotions in that room are what are paramount. They demand to be heard." He walked to the sink and rinsed out his coffee cup. "I'll be there at one. I hope you'll reconsider."

He left her alone. She flinched when she heard the front door slam shut. The uncontrolled action marked his frustration with the situation. Sinking down, she buried her face in her hands and tried to forget his request. She couldn't. The simple truth was her sister needed her, and she couldn't let her down again. If she hadn't pushed Sandra away because of their conflicting views toward what Ian called her talent, she would know about the new man in her sister's life. Anna just didn't believe she had it in her to go through the torment again. Even after fifteen years the hurt was fresh, deep.

***

Anna stared at her sister's front door, feeling as though it were a hundred-foot wall she had to scale. She clenched her hands, causing Sandra's apartment key to dig into her palm, reminding her pain awaited her on the other side.

When the door swung open, she gasped. Ian filled the entrance with his large frame— commanding, intense, as if he were a warrior preparing for battle. Perhaps they both were—her to fight the demons from her past, and him to fight this serial killer preying on women.

"You came."

"How did you know I was out here?"

He shrugged. "A hunch."

Anna raised one eyebrow, not ready to accept his explanation. "Another one of your talents?"

He ignored her comment and turned back into the apartment, leaving the door ajar. She entered and froze in the middle of the hallway, staring into Sandra's living room, glimpsing the edge of the glass coffee table and the navy and tan chair. All she had to do was put one foot in front of the other, but her limbs didn't want to obey her brain's command.

Was Ian right about facing her psychic abilities and learning to control them? Could he help her? Could she allow someone that close? Sandra had tried to help her, and she had rejected her sister's assistance. How could she accept Ian's, a stranger to her until a few days ago?

Take it one step at a time, Anna.

She wasn't sure if she'd thought that or if someone had projected that thought into her mind. The pressure in her chest expanded, making it difficult to breathe. Sweat popped out on her upper lip and forehead. A rivulet rolled down and stung her eye. She wiped the perspiration away and forced herself to walk toward Sandra's living room.

When she stepped into the living room, she half expected to be bombarded with feelings and impressions. But nothing happened. Ian sat on the tan couch, writing something in a note pad. He glanced up, a smile in his eyes.

"I'm glad you came," he said, not moving.

"I don't know why I did." She leaned back against the closed door, seeking some kind of support to keep herself upright.

"Don't lie to yourself any longer, Anna. You know exactly why you're here."

"To help Sandra."

"That may be part of it, but you want to help yourself, too. You've known for years something wasn't right with your life."

She grimaced at the harsh bite to his world weary voice. "My first and only concern is my sister."

"Okay." He pushed off the couch and approached her, hand extended. "Then let's see what we can do to help Sandra."

She eyed him, still not sure she could do what he wanted her to do. "How?"

"You got your strongest feelings when we were in the bedroom the last time. Let's try there."

She ignored the hand he offered and walked past him toward the bedroom. The entrance loomed before her like a black, menacing cave, and she'd never been comfortable in the dark. She stopped, aware he was right behind her. His presence tingled down her length, heightening all her senses.

Even before she stepped into her sister's bedroom, energy swirled around, drawing her forward as though it were a whirlpool sucking her under. Trancelike, she made her way to the bed and stretched out on top of the covers with her arms stiff at her sides, staring at a dust bunny on the white ceiling. From the fringes of her awareness she saw Ian prowl Sandra's personal domain, again touching various objects, running his finger over the clear, clean lines of a jewelry box and the rounded curves of the tan phone on the bedside table. Nothing registered in his expression.

Suddenly air swooshed from her lungs as though someone lay on top of her, pressing her down into the mattress. She couldn't breathe, her chest searing with each attempt. Flinging her arms up as if she could shove the imaginary person from her, she gasped, struggling to sit up. The room spun in ever increasing speed.

Ian stooped down next to her, lifting her up. The pressure eased from about her chest as alien feelings battered at her fragile control—her sister's elation at the new man in her life, her anticipation of the date to come, and her surprise then fear—all swam around in Anna's mind like an emotional kaleidoscope.

She closed her eyes to the reeling room, clasping her temples. She wanted to stop the onslaught. *Too much.* The explosion of emotions inside her threatened her sanity. She shook her head, her hands still gripping it. *No, go away.*

Then there was nothing. Her mind emptied while hearing a man's cry in the throes of passion. It pierced her thoughts like a hot branding iron. With the sound still echoing in her head, Anna slumped over, Ian's arms coming about her to keep her from falling off the bed.

"Anna?"

His voice cut through the numbing sensation seizing her. But she couldn't form any words to respond. She couldn't find the energy even to move. She felt as though she had scaled that hundred foot wall, inch by slow inch.

Ian held Anna against him, helpless to take the pain away. He had forced her to do this, and now he wasn't sure if that had been wise. Placing his palm against her head, he probed her mind, alarmed at its blank slate.

"Anna, listen to my voice." He clutched her arms and shook her gently. When she just stared at him, not responding to him, he jostled her harder. "Anna. Come on. I'm here. Don't give in to it."

He swore beneath his breath, cradled her back against him, and framed her head between his hands. He would have to be careful and make sure his timing was perfect. A faint glow shimmered beneath his skin, growing brighter as he closed his eyes and concentrated on transferring his energy into her.

She jerked, her head dropping forward, her shoulders sagging. Then slowly she lifted her chin, looking about her. "Ian? I—I—"

He wound his arms around her and brought her back against him, resting his chin on the top of her head. "I'm sorry. I pushed you when you weren't ready. I thought if I was here I could keep you grounded."

"I felt everything at once. Such intense emotions, all vying for my attention."

"I know. Before you do it again—"

"No, I can't."

The husky timbre in her voice touched his hardened core. Beneath his arms that crisscrossed her chest her heart pounded so rapidly he was afraid she would faint. "Relax now. Think of something pleasant." He schooled his voice into a gentle monotone. "I will teach you to contain it and control it."

She trembled. "You make it sound so simple. Put it in a box for me to open when I want."

"It is a lot like that. Do you think you can stand?"

She scooted to the edge of the bed and attempted to rise. Immediately she collapsed back and slumped against him. His arms locked about her again.

"We can stay here until you—"

"No," she cut in, her voice frantic. "I can't stay in Sandra's bedroom another moment. Help me."

Her plea tore at the defenses he'd erected over the centuries. Normally he didn't allow humans to touch him, for he'd found that it interfered with him doing his job. But Anna was different. It had been thousands of years since one of his race had been taught how to control his psychic abilities. He wasn't a teacher, but if he wanted Anna's help, he would have to instruct her, much as his sire had him.

He slipped from behind her and stood, then picked her up and carried her out into the living room. The feel of her in his arms spoke to a part of him he wanted to keep hidden. He could get used to holding her. "Is this okay?"

She scanned the area, her gaze clouded with doubts. "I guess so. I feel so weak as if I battled the man, too."

When he settled her on the couch then sat next to her, he nestled her within the crook of his arm. "What happened in there?"

"Sandra tried to fight, but she didn't have a chance. She was asleep when he took her. If I didn't know better, I would say they fought in her dreams."

Glad she couldn't see his face, Ian asked, "Any other impressions? Any idea who this man is?"

"I couldn't get past the emotions bombarding me all at once." Anna twisted about to look at him. "The one overriding feeling I had was how evil the man was. You've got to catch him."

She burrowed deeper into the curve of his arm, a coldness enveloping her as if the man was in the room with her. The way he could slip in and out of her mind, she wouldn't be surprised if he was with her in spirit. That thought sent a tremor through her body.

"Cold?"

"Yes."

Ian rubbed his hand up and down her arm and pressed her as close to him as was possible. "I'm going to take you home when you feel up to it, then stop by and see how your sister is."

"I need to come with you." She started to rise but didn't have the energy.

"No, you need to rest because this evening I'll be back to begin our work."

"So soon?" Her hands quivered as she raised one to brush some hair from her face.

"You're right about the man being evil. I don't want anyone else to die because of him."

"Then I'll be ready." She wished she had more strength behind those words. She wasn't sure she would ever be ready.

***

"You don't look so hot," Terri said to Ian as he came into the hospital room.

"I don't feel so hot, either. I don't particularly like using people, and I did today. I came close to reallly huring her."

"Anna?"

He gave her a curt nod. "I pushed when I knew better, but I'm so close to the Chameleon. I feel his energy. He's still here in Lexington. I know it."

"Maybe you're too close to this one."

Ian slumped onto the couch, hanging his head and kneading the back of his neck. "Probably."

"Then let someone else do this job."

"No! I'm the Protector. There is no one else."

"But I'm sure the Circle can find someone to step in temporarily, especially under the circumstances. You can't allow your emotions to get in your way. We have to be above that."

"Emotions are the problem. That's why I need Anna. She's emotionally connected to the only person who has survived longer than a few days. I can't get a read. Emotions are in the way. I even lied to Anna about how I could feel her sadness. That wasn't what I felt. I felt the conflict, not the emotion. Maybe all those years ago it was a mistake for us to suppress our emotional side. Then maybe I wouldn't need to use Anna like I am."

"She's really getting to you. Why? You've worked

with humans before."

"Not this strong. Not this—" His voice faded into silence. He wasn't able to put his thoughts into words.

"Intriguing, attractive, appealing?"

"Perhaps all of the above."

"That doesn't sound good, Ian. Get out now. Let someone else take over. Maybe I could—"

"No!" He shot to his feet and glared at Terri. "This is not up for discussion. Long ago, the Chameleon's father started this with mine. I will finish it now that he's turned from our ways. He can use the energy he's harvesting to change his appearance, but he won't escape me in the end."

She held up her hand. "Okay. I won't say another word except to warn you to be careful. Anna Stanfield may not be good for you."

"You don't have to tell me that. I already know it." He stared down at Sandra, so calm looking amid the turmoil swirling around inside him. "How many people have visited her?"

"A fair number."

"Anyone suspicious?"

"Only one. A young man. He was quite agitated. He wouldn't tell me his name, and when I probed, his thoughts were in such chaos. I couldn't get a fix on it, so he's probably not the Chameleon."

"You forget that we can disguise our inner thoughts. I'm sure the Chameleon is quite good at that. We could be standing next to him and not know it."

"Which makes it very difficult to find him."

"I will find him. I won't let our race go through another Hunt like the last time."

Terri shivered. "My brother was killed by the humans during that time."

"Hundreds were before we learned to protect ourselves."

"That was thousands of years ago. We've lived in harmony since then."

"Harmony can be unbalanced at any time." Ian walked toward the door. "I'll check back with you later. If anything happens, let me know immediately. I'll be with Anna."

***

He perused the St. Louis airport lounge and found his next victim. She sat at a table by herself, her long legs crossed and her head buried in a book. Her long blonde hair fell forward, hiding part of her face, but he'd seen it. She was beautiful, with full lips and wide, green eyes fringed in dark lashes. He got so excited just thinking about her vitality that he could hardly contain his glow of energy.

"Excuse me. Is this seat taken?" he asked the blonde beauty.

She glanced up from her paperback and scanned the other empty chairs nearby. As a frown creased her brow, he reached into her thoughts and commanded she ask him to sit.

"No," she answered, gesturing for him to take the chair next to her.

"I see you're reading the latest John Sandford novel."

"Yes, do you like him?"

"I've read several of his earlier works. When's your flight?"

"Not for a few hours."

"Mine isn't until this evening. I hate waiting in airports." He delved into her mind, planting a message of mutual attraction. Normally he allowed a natural affinity to develop, but he didn't have the time today.

"Me, too." She leaned forward, closing the book and placing it on the table. Her attention was totally focused on him now. "There's nothing to help pass the time except reading."

"I can think of something much more entertaining."

He took her hand, stroking it.

Her eyes grew round. "The airport hotel isn't too far."

He rose, helping her out of her chair. His skin tingled with awareness of the woman beside him as they strode through the airport. The energy she generated expanded, enticing him even more to feed, even though he didn't need to. She was so perfect. A wonderful appetizer. But Anna would be his meal.

When they arrived at the airport hotel, she offered to get the room after he'd silently suggested it to her. He stood by the bank of elevators, keeping people away until they'd ridden upstairs.

In the nondescript room he backed her up against the wall just inside the door and ravished her mouth, tasting peppermint on her tongue. Covering her breast with a hand, he could tell she wanted it quick and hard. That suited him just fine. He tore at the buttons on her blouse, hearing one pop off and hit the tiled entrance.

Her chest heaved, her breasts swelling beneath the lacy bits of the bra. Unsnapping the front clasp, he slid the straps down her arms, then took a puckered nipple into his mouth and suckled. Her moan spurred him to give equal attention to the other one.

Her hands went to his belt and fumbled, unfastening it. He stilled her movements and maneuvered her toward the bed. Shoving her down onto the mattress, he quickly undressed, then helped her out of the rest of her clothes. The whole time he sent hot signals of desire to her until he saw her eyes glaze over and her breathing become erratic.

He came down on top of her and entered her all the way with one thrust, relishing her cry of pleasure. Plunging in and out, he quickened his pace, releasing himself deep inside her. She screamed again. At the peak of her elation, he placed his hands on her head and pinned her to the mattress.

He began to glow with a blinding light. Through his fingertips his spirit soared into her body and spread to all reaches, drawing her life force to him. When he emptied her vessel, she died.

He roared with his triumph, even though it was short lived. The second he rolled off her the restlessness crashed into him. She hadn't been enough. After Sandra, he wanted someone with a high degree of psychic ability—the more the better. That would be the closest he could come to raping a member of his own race, which was an impossibility. He wanted to destroy the Cintarians as clearly as they had destroyed his family. He would have his revenge he mentally shouted for all Cintarians to hear.

Come and get me, Hawk.

Seven

The Chameleon's words flooded Ian's thoughts, obliterating everything else. He grabbed hold of Anna's porch railing, sinking against it, and forced his heart to calm its racing beat. The Chameleon's intention invaded every pore, leaving Ian little doubt that time was running out. Pushing himself away from the railing, he headed for the door, pressing the bell.

Anna dragged herself up from the couch, the word revenge echoing through her mind much like the doorbell was through her house. Shaking the sleep from her mind, she hurried toward the door, and after peering out the peephole, opened it.

"How's Sandra?" she asked, raking her hand through her hair.

Ian came into the house. "No change."

She sagged back against the door. "I suppose that's better than she's worse. I need to go see her, but—" She couldn't finish her sentence. No words could describe the exhausted feeling she was experiencing.

"I'll take you up after our lesson." He walked into the living room, leaving her in the entrance hall.

The energy vibrating from him called to her. She reluctantly followed, not looking forward to her lesson, not after the session at Sandra's. "I've slept all day, but I'm still wiped out."

"I'd love to rush this, but we can't, so this first lesson

won't be as taxing mentally. Sit down. Relax."

"You say that a lot to me."

He grinned. "It's important. Stress interferes with the process."

"Then I'm not sure this is a good time to teach me."

"We have to work with what we have. If I waited for a less stressful time in your life, there wouldn't be a need to do this."

Anna took a seat on the couch, aware there was room for him beside her.

He stood in the middle of the living room. "Are you comfortable?"

She nodded. His energy charged the air as though tiny bolts of electricity emanated from him.

"Good. I want you to take deep breaths, and when you inhale think of unlocking your heart and letting it expand. When you exhale, let go of any concerns you have. Good thoughts in, bad thoughts out."

She did as he instructed, not sure what he meant by unlocking her heart. For the moment she tried to forget about Sandra and the man after her. She tried to dismiss her natural wariness and embrace life with a wholeheartedness.

"Clear your mind, Anna. Believe in yourself and your abilities. You have a special gift that can help people."

His words calmed the ruffled edges of the doubt hovering in her thoughts like a black cloud. She emptied her mind of all the trash that cluttered it.

He crossed the room and sat next to her. "I want you to create for yourself a sacred space, a place where you can direct your psychic abilities. You can use an image, a sound, whatever works for you. I want you to be able to come and go at will into this space."

She thought of opening a door and stepping into a room full of bright light, warm and nurturing.

"At the beginning you need to state your intentions. Shed the mundane world for the spiritual."

"My intention is to find who hurt my sister."

Anna blinked. Ice invaded her veins, the warm, nurturing light gone. All calmness fled, the spell Ian wove broken. She let out a rush of air through pursed lips. Tension blanketed her, causing her to sit straighter on the couch, her shoulders thrown back, her jaw clamped shut.

"What I want for you is a safe place for you to go so if you need to retreat you can. I want you to be able to control your abilities—not let them control you. There are certain things you need to do to ready yourself, or you'll find the ordinary world keeps you grounded in it."

A slow cadence masked Ian's impatience, but Anna saw it in the deep lines of his forehead, a shadow in his dark eyes. "How can I unlock and expand my heart, as you say? I don't trust easily."

"It's about empathy and human connectedness."

"I'm supposed to forget all my worries and pretend nothing bad happened to Sandra? I can't do that."

"You need to be emotionally available, and stress interferes with that."

"Emotionally available! I think that's my problem. I'm too wrapped up in Sandra's emotions. I can't weed through them to discover the man who caused them."

Ian gripped her hands, twisting her around to face him. "I'm not talking about your sister's emotions. I'm talking about yours. I'm talking about being receptive to your psychic abilities and controlling them so they don't overwhelm you." Frustrated, he released her and jackknifed to his feet. "I'm not the one to teach you this. It's been years—" He glanced down at her, something flickering in his gaze.

"Years what? Have you had training in this?"

"Not everyone grew up as you did, unschooled in the

ways of psi. I had a mentor."

"You did? Who?"

"My father."

"Your father was psychic?"

"Yes, and very likely there was someone in your family who was, too."

Anna thought of her family. "My grandmother was rumored to be strange. She died when I was five, so I didn't know her very well."

"I wish we had more time. This isn't something that should be rushed."

He paced the room, touching different objects as though trying to get a read on her through her possessions. On a bookcase filled with psychology books, he picked up a statue of an angel, then another one. "You collect angels? What's rational and logical about angels?"

"I never said everything I did was rational and logical. It's something I used to do as a little girl, and I still do." Angry at her defensive tone, she tilted up her chin and squared her shoulders until her back ached.

"Ah, so there is a whimsical side to you."

"How did you become an FBI agent?" she asked, preferring to discuss him rather than her. She already felt that her life wasn't hers anymore, that people were tramping around in her mind, leaving her vulnerable and open.

"My hunches have been a guide for me. They can be for you, too. Your abilities aren't a burden but a gift."

"That may be easy for you to say, but you didn't grow up in a town that feared you. I don't want this gift you say I have."

He sighed and knelt down in front of her, taking her hands. "You may not have a choice."

"People always have choices."

"I can help you to see it as a gift, but you'll have to

trust me to be your guide."

"I thought I wasn't supposed to trust anyone, even you."

"I was wrong."

She laughed. "I suspect that might be the only time I hear you say those words."

His smile transformed his serious expression into a sexy one that prodded her heart to beat faster. Suddenly, all she could think about was his hands on her. She'd never been with a man who liked to touch as much as he did, as though that physical connection was important to him. Perhaps it was, she thought, remembering what he had said his talent was.

He cupped her face. "You may be right, so enjoy it while you can."

His gaze linked with hers. She became lost in his midnight dark eyes as he tugged her toward him. His mouth feathered across hers, his touch like the caress of a gentle summer breeze, almost elusive. She wound her arm about him, seeking more than a brush of his lips, suddenly wanting to capture all of him.

This time when his mouth settled over hers, it was a demanding kiss that sought to bind them together as though they were fused. The sensations he created shattered her fragile control. Every sense sharpened. While she drowned in the musky scent of him, she tasted his mint-flavored toothpaste on her tongue and perceived the silkiness of his hair beneath her fingertips, the roughness of his cheek against hers. But above everything else she felt as if he'd enclosed them in a glass bubble, shutting out the world.

He groaned and pulled back, the glass bubble shattering. "I didn't mean for that to happen."

"But it did."

"Yes." He rose, towering over her. He looked long

and hard at her, then pivoted and headed for the door. "I'll be back tomorrow morning, and we'll begin again."

The sound of him leaving brought Anna out of her daze. She hugged her arms to herself, suddenly cold as if his departure had taken the warmth from the room, too. The feel of his lips on hers burned into her mind. What was happening to her? Her life was no longer hers to command.

***

Ian sat cross-legged in the middle of his hotel suite's living room, his arms relaxed on his knees, spine straight, shoulders back. What was happening to him? He'd lost control and kissed her. Emotions had almost gotten in his way, and becoming involved with Anna Stanfield was definitely not a good idea.

He took a deep breath then another, filling his lungs until he thought they would burst. Closing his eyes, he pulled inward, forming a small ball of energy that escaped its bodily restraints and soared upward.

He called to his uncle, beckoning him to appear. Light blazed around him, surrounding him in a protective shell. "Uncle, I'm at a loss about what to do with Anna Stanfield. I have never mentored."

"She is strong?"

"Yes, with many of our abilities."

"She has a lot of Cintarian blood in her."

"But most of her life she's suppressed her psi, even denying it exists. I need her help in identifying the Chameleon's new persona. He's still here. She's my connection to Sandra."

"Do not push. It won't come when you do. She must be totally relaxed and completely trust you. Think back to your father's teachings."

For once fear of failure clawed at Ian's heart. His resolve wavered.

"You have always succeeded, but be careful. I sense an increase in your emotional energy. You can't afford that. Our emotions betrayed us once. No human must know of our existence. They would not take kindly to us if they knew about our powers."

The brightness of the light dimmed, and the protective shell faded. Ian sank back into himself, slowly opening his eyes. He wasn't sure he was any closer to helping Anna, but the comfort he derived from connecting with his uncle eased his apprehension. He would start again with Anna first thing tomorrow morning.

***

I'm coming, Anna. I'm near, and you won't escape me.

Anna's eyes popped open, and she jerked up in the easy chair. The sound of laughter reverberated in her mind, and for a few seconds she wasn't sure who was laughing. An *I Love Lucy* rerun was showing on the television. She snatched up the remote and clicked off the set.

Not moving, hardly even breathing, she listened. Only silence greeted her. She relaxed back in the chair, deciding she had been dreaming again. Switching off the lamp next to her, she drew solace from the dim light filtering through the slit in the drawn curtains.

Dawn, the time of day she loved best. Spring, the time of year she loved best. The staleness of the indoor air lured her outside to welcome the new day. She shoved to her feet and went into the kitchen. After brewing a pot of coffee, she took her large yellow mug and strode out onto the back deck.

Lounging in a white wicker chair, she sipped her coffee and drank in the beauty surrounding her. Streaks of gold, orange and rose fanned out from the horizon, pushing the darkness back. Birds sang in the oak and maple trees in her yard while a light breeze ruffled strands of her hair.

Perfect. Tranquil. Just what she needed. She sighed and snuggled back into the deep, forest green cushion, relishing the taste of coffee as it slid down her throat.

Anna, you can't run from me.

She stiffened, clenching her mug as she brought it down from her mouth.

I'm here. Watching.

She hated her need to scan her backyard, but she did. The dark shadows lingered near the crop of trees along her property line that edged an alley. The sensation of eyes mauling her body knocked the breath from her, squeezing her heart in a vise. She stumbled to her feet, coffee scalding her hand. The mug crashed to the deck, the sound taunting her as she twisted about to race for the safety of her house.

See Anna run.

She clawed at the door, trying to get inside. A fingernail broke, shooting pain up her arm. Finally the knob turned, and she wrenched the door open and rushed inside. She threw the deadbolt into place. Sucking in gasps of air, she yanked open drawer after drawer until she found a weapon—a long butcher knife.

Do you think that will hurt me?

"No!"

She clutched the knife and hurried into the living room, whirling about as if the man was in her house. Her pulse roared in her ears, momentarily drowning out her harsh breathing. Again she spun around in a full circle, searching the dark corners. While her heart sped, she took a step back toward the entrance into the hallway, the knife held out in front of her.

When the doorbell rang, she jumped, nearly dropping the weapon. She pivoted toward the foyer, the rasp of her breathing so loud that she wondered if she'd really heard her doorbell.

When I take you—

"No, stop it!" she screamed, releasing the knife which clattered when it hit the tile floor. She clasped her ears to still the voice inside her head.

"Anna, are you all right," Ian shouted, pounding on the front door. "Open up. Now." He pressed the bell over and over.

Ian. Here. That realization worked its way into her frantically racing mind. Dropping her arms, she rushed to the door. At the last second she checked to make sure it was Ian before jerking it open. She fell into his arms, tears clogging her throat.

He took her into his embrace, hugging her close to him. She felt his steady heartbeat, and hers calmed its frenzied pace. Tears crowded her eyes and spilled down her cheeks. Safe. For now.

"Anna, what happened?" He cradled her to his side and walked her into the house. "You had a knife. Why?" He stared at the weapon on the floor.

"He's after me."

"He's here?" Ian pushed her behind him and withdrew his gun. "Why didn't—"

"No, he's not in the house—at least I don't think so."

Still shielding her with his body, his gaze searching the area, he asked, "What do you mean?"

"I heard him."

"He called you?"

"No, he spoke to me in my mind." Anna groaned, clasping her head again. "I sound crazy."

Ian spun around to face Anna, gripping her arms and forcing her to look at him. "You aren't crazy."

"People don't speak to people through their thoughts."

Anna, I can speak to you that way.

"He's doing it again! Make him stop." She shook her head as if that would rid her of the voice.

"Anna, I just spoke to you. It wasn't him."

Her mouth fell open. She stepped back against the door, her eyes wide. "He's psychic?"

Ian nodded, moving close. "Very strong."

"Why didn't you tell me this?"

"Because I didn't want to frighten you any more than you are."

"I deserve to know everything about this case." Anger seized her, and she shoved him away. "What else are you keeping from me?"

"Was this the first time he's contacted you?"

"No, but you didn't answer—"

"When did he contact you before?" Fury flashed into Ian's dark eyes as he closed the space between them. "Why didn't you tell me?"

"Because I didn't believe it."

"What has he said?" His fingers dug into the flesh of her upper arms.

She squeezed her eyes closed for a few seconds before facing Ian's wrath. "The bottom line is, he wants me. He's coming after me."

Ian swore beneath his breath. Releasing her, he snatched up the knife and strode toward the kitchen. Exhausted, worried, frustrated, Anna stormed after him, wanting a fight.

"None of this is my fault. I didn't ask for this." Her voice rose with each word.

Ian pivoted, his gaze cutting through her. "All this time he's been sending you messages, and you didn't tell me. You realize you're as much in danger as your sister?"

The knowledge she could be lying in the hospital, or worse the morgue, slammed into her with such force she clutched the back of the chair to steady herself. She'd focused on Sandra's plight and had thrust hers to the background. Sitting, she pressed her palms to her face, wishing she could hide from the world.

Ian's fingers began working the tautness loose in her shoulders. "I know this is hard for you."

The controlled calmness in his voice ripped away all her defenses. Her tears flowed. "I don't know what to do anymore. I thrive on order and some kind of control of my life. I have neither at the moment."

Easing down into the chair next to her, Ian scooted it toward her. "You realize I will have to stay here."

"No, you can't!" Alarm clamored a warning.

"You have to be guarded as closely as your sister."

"I can take—"

He brushed his fingers across her lips to seal her words inside. "This man is very dangerous, deadly. He could be anybody. A supposed friend. A student in your class. Your neighbor."

Defeat made her shoulders sag.

"You needn't worry. This arrangement will be strictly professional."

Anna remembered the kiss and couldn't shake the feeling she didn't want it to be professional. Yet, any involvement would complicate the situation.

"Go get ready, and you can come with me while I pack my things and check out of the hotel." He rose and offered her his hand. "This might be for the better anyway. We need to work on your lessons, and this way we can do so more often."

Anna stood, avoiding the lure of his hand. Halfway to the door his next words stopped her.

"I need to know every time he contacts you— *immediately.*"

Slanting a look over her shoulder, Anna frowned. "Often it's when I'm sleeping. That's why I didn't think it was real at first. I'm still not totally convinced it is."

"It's real, Anna. And when you're sleeping, you're at

your most vulnerable. All your defenses are at their weakest level."

"That's reassuring. I may never sleep again."

He strode to her. "I'll be here. You'll be all right so long as you let me know." His smile curved his mouth. "Go get dressed."

***

"Okay, we're going to try something different this time."

Seated on her couch, Anna eyed Ian warily. The darkness beyond the window heightened her anxiety. They had been working all day, and she still felt no closer to what he wanted from her.

"You need to be completely relaxed. As stress free as possible."

"Isn't that going to be a little hard?"

"I realize the circumstances aren't ideal—"

"I'd say they were lousy."

He grimaced. "Yeah, well, we don't have a lot of control over the situation."

"You can say that again. We have no control."

Moving behind the couch, Ian drew Anna back. "I want you to clear your mind of all thoughts. Concentrate on my hands and what they're doing."

Their massaging motion guaranteed she would think of nothing but his hands. They kneaded the tight muscles in her neck and shoulders with such expert deliberation. Her eyelids slid closed as a sigh of appreciation whispered past her lips. Maybe this was what she needed.

He worked her neck loose, then slipped down her spine to rub under her shoulder blades. "What's your favorite place? The one that gives you the most comfort."

She thought of her backyard that morning and the feelings she'd had right before the man had contacted her. "A walled garden with hundreds of flowers in bloom and tall trees for shade. The grass is lush, cool to the touch. There's a fountain, and the sound of water gurgling soothes me. Butterflies and birds abound. Huge goldfish swim in the pool that is fed by the fountain."

"Go there in your mind." He came around the couch and knelt in front of her. "Take off your shoes." He removed hers, his fingers branding her skin. "Bury your toes in the grass. Wiggle them. Feel the coolness. Feel the blades sensually caress your feet." Taking one foot, Ian applied pressure to the bottom of it, then massaged it.

She should open her eyes. Tell him to stop. How could this help her find her sister's attacker?

"Clear your mind. You're tensing up again. Go back to your walled garden. Trust me."

She gave in to the feel of his fingers pressing into her flesh. She returned to her haven, savoring the sun on her face, the sounds—flowing water, birds chirping—the peacefulness, the security.

"Ah, that's much better."

The touch of his hands slid up her legs, rubbing her calves. She collapsed back on the couch, every muscle drained.

"Now imagine me in your walled garden."

She never shared—

"Let me in, Anna. Only you can control who comes into your sacred place." He took her hand and kneaded the palm, his voice a husky whisper.

He materialized in her sanctuary. His head tossed back, he welcomed the caress of the sun as she had. The carefree look on his face transformed his serious expression. The gleam in his eyes melted any reservations she had for allowing him into her world.

In her mind he strode to her and held both her hands between them. *Anna, create a door in the wall so you can go in and out.* He looked toward the red bricks forming the barrier to the outside world. She pictured a gate, and one appeared where she stared.

This is your way out when things get too much for you. All you have to do is walk through that gate. You control it. You'll be safe.

Control it? Be safe? How? Someone's after me and Sandra. Her walled garden vanished like the illusion it was.

Anna opened her eyes. Ian wiped the frown from his expression, but she saw the concern in his features before he masked it.

"I'm sorry. This isn't easy for me."

"Letting someone else in? Or, thinking yourself safe, in control?"

"Up until recently I would have said the letting someone else in. Now, I think it is both of those reasons." A dull ache throbbed behind her eyes. She winced and clasped her temples.

"Here, let me try to get rid of your headache."

She shook away his offer and forced herself to her feet. "No, I think some aspirin will work just fine."

Hurrying from the room, she escaped into the bathroom, and after putting the toilet top down, sat. She scrubbed her fingertips down her face, trying to rid herself of the sensation of being possessed. But for a few minutes she'd let him into her refuge. Shocked at how easily he was becoming important to her, she banished from her thoughts the delight she'd experienced. Nothing in her life was as it seemed. Up was down, and in was out. She had to remember that.

A knock sounded at the door. "Are you all right, Anna?"

She rose. "Fine. I'll be out in a second."

She rummaged around in the medicine cabinet until she found some aspirin and took two. When she opened the door, Ian lounged against the opposite wall, arms folded across his chest, worry creasing his brow.

"I'm fine. Really. Just tired."

"It's probably time for both of us to go to bed. Where do you want me to sleep?"

The question threw her off guard for a moment. She blinked, glancing at the three bedroom doors down the hallway. "I have a guest bedroom you can use. It's next to mine." *Now, why did I say that?* She blushed.

"Good. I'll go out to the car and bring in my bags."

While he was gone, she quickly gathered some towels for him to use and placed them on his bed. When she turned to leave, he stood just inside the door, a smoldering look in his dark eyes that stole her breath. He veiled his expression and carried his two pieces of luggage into the room.

"I'm a light sleeper. If anything unusual happens, let me know immediately."

She backed herself toward the door. "I'm sure I'll be perfectly fine with you here to protect me."

"Anna," he called out.

She paused at the door.

"Don't underestimate the threat to you. This man is very dangerous and will stop at nothing to get what he wants."

"With those words, I'm sure I'll sleep well tonight."

He lifted one bag onto the bed and opened it. "If it will make you feel safer, I can sleep in your bedroom."

The thought of him in the next room was bad enough. "No, I think I'll pass on that offer."

"Then sweet dreams," Ian said as he unpacked his clothes.

Anna strode the few feet to her bedroom and ducked inside. Just seeing him putting his things into the drawers made her heart gallop. He would be sleeping in her house for an indefinite amount of time. The realization spread a wave of heat throughout her body, and she sank down onto her bed, falling back to stare at the ceiling.

She was placing her trust in a stranger. She didn't even totally trust friends. Why Ian McGregory?

The question plagued her as she prepared for bed. The answer wasn't any closer when she slipped between the cool sheets and laid her head on her soft pillow.

For the first hour she rolled over and punched her pillow as though that would help her to sleep. She didn't want to, but exhaustion clung to every inch of her. If she was going to be any help to Sandra, she needed to rest.

The red number on the digital clock proclaimed a few minutes past midnight. She twisted onto her right side. A couple of minutes later she flipped over onto her back and stared at the dark ceiling.

Staying awake won't keep me out, Anna.

She jerked up in bed, scanning the blackness.

I'm coming for you.

Bolting out of bed, she raced from her bedroom and burst into Ian's. "He's here!"

Eight

Gun in hand, Ian sprang from his bed. The moonlight streamed in through the open curtains, revealing him alert, scanning the darkness as though he could see. But for a few seconds all Anna could focus on was the fact he only wore his boxer shorts. Transfixed, she stared at his powerful body.

Run, Anna, run.

Her breath froze in her throat. *Leave me alone.*

As fast as you can.

Panic ripped through her, urging her forward. She fled across the room and threw herself at Ian. He captured her to him with one arm while still holding the gun, his gaze continuing to sweep the area.

"I heard," he said, such a cold, steel thread in his voice that Anna shivered. "But he isn't in the house."

"How can you tell?" Another tremor shook her, her tension as thick as his.

"I just can. He's toying with you, trying to keep you rattled."

She buried herself in the crook of his arm, listening to the beat of his heart, a shade faster than usual. The rhythmic sound soothed her tattered nerves and quieted her own frantically racing one. "I feel like I'm being hunted."

"You are."

What calmness she'd gathered dissipated with those

words. "If I wasn't so tired, I'd—" She couldn't finish her bogus threat because she didn't know what she would do. She felt helpless against this unknown killer lurking in her mind, stalking her in its dark recesses. That was absurd, but she couldn't rid herself of that sensation.

"He wants you off kilter, exhausted, hysterical."

"Well, I hate to tell you, but his plan is working. I haven't slept well since Sandra went into a coma, and these past few nights have been the worst."

Ian laid his gun on the bedside table. "Then stay with me tonight. I'll make sure he doesn't bother you while you're sleeping."

She leaned back, trying to fathom the intentions behind his words. Moonlight illuminated nothing in his features except steely determination to protect. *Safe.* The word blanketed her mind, reaching into those dark recesses to chase away the killer's threat, to erase any trace of his presence, imagined or real.

"I don't know if I can sleep. The dreams." She shuddered. "What can you do?" she asked, desperation in her question.

"Protect you."

Those simple words, spoken in a fierce tone, convinced her she would be safe from the killer—and from Ian. But she wasn't worried so much about Ian as herself. He had such tight control over his desires and emotions, whereas she was losing what control she'd had. He made her feel things she'd never thought possible. How was she going to share a bed with him and get any sleep? Even in the midst of all this terror she wanted to experience more than his kiss.

"You have to get some rest, or what you and I are doing won't work. I can help you."

"You've been saying that a lot lately."

"All part of the job."

"But this isn't part of your job. The FBI doesn't consider this a case."

"Once you've sworn to protect, Anna, there are no boundaries to that. Case or no case, this is my job."

"Okay, you've convinced me. You may have your way with me."

He chuckled, the sound lightening the mood. "Now that's an interesting comment."

"I meant you can help me," she said, flustered, feeling the heat of a blush scorch her cheeks. "If you know how to get me to sleep, short of knocking me out, then I'm game. See, that's my exhaustion talking."

He guided her to the double bed and pulled back the covers. "Lie down. That's the first step."

"Said the spider to the fly," she mumbled and slid between the coolness of the sheets, now conscious that all she wore was a flimsy nightgown. Why hadn't she dressed in the flannel pajamas she wore during the winter?

She shifted, trying to get comfortable. When he joined her on the bed, she tensed. "Can't you sleep on the floor? In the chair?"

"Not for what I want to do."

"What?" Her voice cracked as she scooted to a sitting position next to him.

In the suddenly small bed—why wasn't this a king-sized one—her arm brushed against his, sending tingles through her. A finely honed tension twisted her stomach muscles into a compressed knot.

"Relax," Ian said, humor vibrating in his voice. "All I want to do is hold you."

"Why?"

"You are full of questions tonight. Trust me. I can help you sleep. And if you ask how, I'm sending you back to your room."

The laughter in his voice eased some of her

apprehension, until he wrapped his arm about her and tugged her up against him. Then it returned full force.

"I don't have to read your mind to know what's running through yours about now. Believe me, that is the furthest thing from mine."

"Reassuring but not very flattering."

"Do you want me to flatter you?"

The amusement in his question made her want to punch him in the stomach. "No, of course not." She tried to sound perturbed, but all she managed was a breathless answer.

He adjusted her so her body curled into his side. With her head lying on his shoulder, he rested his chin on the top of her hair. "I like your shampoo. It smells like jasmine."

"That's not flattery."

"I know. I was just making conversation, getting you to relax. If you get any stiffer, I'm afraid you'll break from the strain. And like Humpty Dumpty, I don't think I could put you back together again."

This was ridiculous, Anna thought. It wasn't as if she'd never been in bed with a man. Granted her experiences were limited, but they were both adults and could control themselves. She decided to practice a relaxation technique he'd taught her. She took a deep breath and released it slowly over and over until her tension slackened.

"Somehow I don't see you reading Mother Goose nursery rhymes," she told him.

"What do you see me reading?"

"Adventure thrillers?"

He chuckled. "No, I don't have the time. When I do read, it's all nonfiction. How about you?"

"The same. I do a lot to stay current in my field." She burrowed closer.

"Do you like to teach?"

"Yes. I fell into teaching. Never thought I would enjoy it because I would have to actually get up in front of people. But I love psychology and love talking about it, so getting up in front of my class is the easy part. How about you? What made you join the FBI?"

"It just seemed logical, considering my interests."

"What are they?"

"The criminal mind. What makes people do what they do."

"That's psychology."

"Then we have a lot in common."

The statement hung between them as though until that moment neither one had realized that. "Yes, we do," Anna finally said.

Silence fell. A tree branch scraping against the house, a lone dog next door barking—probably at the cat from across the street—were the only sounds Anna heard. Her mind clicked with one thought after another.

She voiced one out loud. "Where did you grow up?"

"In the mountains."

The slight tensing of his body spoke more than his words. "Did you have a happy childhood?"

"Yes."

Longing laced his answer, underscoring a pain kept buried. "How about you?"

"You know about my childhood, the trouble I had."

"I know the facts, but there's always more than that."

"I think the facts say a lot. I was considered the town freak. To a teenager that is devastating."

"That's devastating to anyone. No one likes to be different. Most people want to quietly go about their business, not be bothered by others."

She pulled back to stare up into his face, shadowed by the night. She wanted to ask what had happened to him to put that world-weary edge into his voice. But something held the words inside.

"You need to go to sleep. It's after one, Anna. Tomorrow we have a lot to do." He cupped her face with one hand and pressed her head to his shoulder. His palm still lay against her cheek, a warm reminder of his appeal.

"I'll try, but like a watched pot doesn't boil, I don't know if I can sleep."

"Take more deep breaths. In with the good. Out with the bad."

She did as he instructed, but all she managed to do was inhale his musky scent, which set off alarms in her mind. "I don't think it's going to work."

"Shh." His fingers in her hair rubbed circles into her scalp.

She focused on their movement—slow, rhythmic like his heartbeat. *Safe.* The word unfurled to every part of her. Her tension drained away. Her mind felt heavy, her eyes burning with exhaustion. She closed them and gave in to the delicious feel of his hand on her head. An image of her walled garden seeped into her thoughts, spreading tranquility like a fog fingering out from a river.

Anna's natural resistance made it difficult for Ian to influence her. But her weariness finally took over and allowed him into her mind. He flooded her thoughts with soothing pictures while planting the idea of security in the middle of them.

He knew the second she succumbed to sleep. She snuggled even closer, as if she were trying to become a part of him. He fought the strong urge to delve deeper into her mind while she was most vulnerable and open. Hundreds of years of training kept him away from her innermost thoughts. For one small moment he could understand the Chameleon's fascination with knowing a person completely. However, while merging with humans was acceptable, stealing their life force and leaving them nothing was inexcusable. And against all Cintarian laws.

Ian shifted so he could enclose Anna in his arms while positioning her head on his chest. When he looked at her in the pale stream of moonlight, his groin tightened. Her secrets, forged in pain, lured him. He'd never merged with anyone totally, not even Miranda, the only woman he'd ever married. Merging would leave him as defenseless as his mate. He'd been the Protector too long to allow that.

Resting his chin on the top of Anna's head, he settled in for a long night. The closer he was physically, the easier it was for him to intercept any communication the Chameleon directed at her. Determination locked his jaw into a hard line. She would sleep uninterrupted. Ian needed her. She was the key.

***

"Come on. Just one cup of coffee, Ian. We can't stay in my house all day." Anna opened the door to Molly's Cafe, the aromas of fried food, brewing coffee and baking bread assailing her, drawing her into her favorite haunt.

"We haven't. We went to see Sandra."

"Another hour, please." She turned toward him, moving so close she could smell his clean, fresh scent. "I need a break. I can only practice relaxing so much."

Ian cracked a smile. "I'm not the warden, Anna. You can leave your house at any time."

"Then coffee and dessert it is." She twisted back around and scanned the restaurant, spotting David and Sloan at a table with two graduate students. "Let's sit over there with them. I want to introduce you to two of my colleagues."

He clasped her arm and came up behind her to whisper into her ear, "Don't let anyone know why I'm really with you."

His breath brushed her neck, sending goose bumps down her spine. "Who are you then?"

"A friend—a very good friend visiting from out of town. I'll let you come up with the rest."

The husky way he'd said friend left little doubt what kind of relationship he wanted projected. The idea of them being lovers heated her pulse. "Okay, I'll play along. But David knows me pretty well. He's going to wonder why I never said anything about you."

"I have every confidence that you'll think of the right thing to say." Ian settled his hand on the small of her back and guided her toward the table in the corner.

"I'm surprised to see you here on Monday, Anna." David shifted to another chair so she and Ian could sit together.

"I just can't stay away, even on the days I don't have classes."

"Flattery will get you everywhere with me, Anna my dear." While eyeing Ian, Sloan waved the waitress over to the table.

After ordering, she introduced Ian to the group. "He's visiting. We went to college together and haven't seen each other in a few years."

David scrutinized Ian. "Staying long?"

Ian placed his arm along the back of Anna's chair. "That depends on some things."

"Oh, the man of mystery. I tried to perfect that and couldn't. What you see is what you get." With a grin, Sloan spread his arms wide.

Anna sent Ian a dreamy look—at least she hoped it was dreamy—for the benefit of the group. Curiosity and even a touch of hostility swirled about the table. Did Sloan or David want more in his relationship with her? Anna wondered, the thought surprising her since neither one had ever indicated that.

She ran her fingers up Ian's arm. "We were *very* good friends in college. It's been nice getting reacquainted."

"Especially with what's happened to your sister. Heaven knows, you need something to take your mind off her accident." Sloan paused while the waitress put two mugs of coffee on the table and one piece of chocolate fudge cake. "How's Sandra?"

"The same." Anna picked up her fork, clutching it to keep her fingers from quivering. "I suppose no news is better than bad news."

"Do the doctors have any idea what happened?" one of the graduate students asked.

"Not a clue." Anna slid a bite of cake into her mouth and savored the chocolate.

"You would think with all our technology they could discover what Sandra's problem is." David frowned, his worried gaze fastened on Anna.

"The brain is a complex organ. We've only begun to understand it," Sloan started in, expounding on some of the advances made in the past decade concerning brain research.

David rolled his eyes. "Dr. Reed, you aren't in your classroom. *Please* give us a break."

Anna laughed. "Actually, I think what he says is interesting. Just think what we could do if we only utilized five or ten percent more of our brain."

"Anyone that did would be considered superhuman. His abilities would be astonishing." Sloan reached over and took a piece of Anna's cake.

Ian stiffened. His tension enveloped Anna, conveying his displeasure at Sloan's casual gesture. He had the part of jealous lover down pat, she noticed when she saw his eyes narrow and his mouth tighten into a thin line. Even a nerve in his jaw twitched.

"What do you do, McGregory?" David asked, diffusing the tense moment.

"I'm in law enforcement."

For a few seconds silence reigned at the table before Sloan lifted a brow. "A policeman?"

"Something like that."

"The man of mystery again." Sloan caught the waitress's attention and indicated he needed the check.

"Actually it's not a mystery. I work for the FBI in the computer area."

"Now you've blown that mystery element right out of the water. Computers have a certain nerd factor."

Anna nearly choked on her coffee at Sloan's statement. She knew he could be outrageous, but it was as though he were going out of his way to be so today.

"But there are so many of us nerds nowadays. Computers have become quite necessary in our society in the last decade."

The humor in Ian's voice challenged Sloan to deny it. He leaned forward, an eager expression on his face. "Sad but true."

"I'm surprised you say that, Reed," David jumped into the conversation. "Where would your research be without the computer?"

"I'm afraid you've done it," Anna whispered into Ian's ear.

He relaxed back, pulling Anna near him, while the rest of the people at the table took sides on the issue of what role computers should play in society. "You learn a lot about people when they debate."

His words tickled the skin beneath her ear. She was the one who studied human nature, but all of a sudden she felt as though Ian was the expert and each of them was under a microscope. She studied each person as he elaborated on his views, trying to see her friends and colleagues through Ian's eyes.

David's passion was shown in his ardent expression, while his quiet words held a steel quality to them. Sloan's intensity undercut his boyish charm. Neither man backed down from his position, which didn't surprise Anna. But their beliefs did. Sloan was the scientist and realist, whereas David was the romantic dreamer. For Sloan to question society's dependency on the computer was out of character. That conclusion made Anna question other conclusions she had about the two men.

Don't trust anyone. Ian's words came back to haunt her. And yet, he was asking her to put her complete trust in him in order to connect with Sandra. His intense focus on the conversation reminded Anna never to let down her guard, even around him.

***

The softness of her bed beckoned. Anna warily stared at her green and gold coverlet, then at Ian next to her. "You want me to do what?"

"Sit on the bed with me."

"And?"

Ian settled onto the coverlet and patted the area in front of him. "And we are going to pair heart-to-heart."

"Pair?" A blush singed her cheeks.

"Come on. Let me show you what I mean. For the past two days you have been resisting me and what I'm trying to do. This will hopefully help you surrender."

"I'm not sure I like the words you're using. Pairing. Surrendering."

"I promise we can stop at any time should you feel threatened."

She eased down in front of him, and he scooted back into the middle of the king size bed, pulling her with him. Sitting with her back plastered against his chest and encased by his strong, powerful legs, Anna tensed.

"Tsk. Tsk. Anna, this isn't going to work if you don't relax. I thought you understood that by now."

His heat seeped into her, surrounding her, tempting

her to drop her defenses. Afraid of his power, she resisted.

"Sandra needs you. I need you."

His whispered words flowed down the column of her neck, sending flutters dancing along her spine. Her defenses crumbled. She nestled against him, her tension melting in the heat of his body.

"I want you to take deep breaths. In with the good, out with the bad."

She did as he requested, thinking about each breath as she inhaled then released it through pursed lips.

"Good. Now imagine your walled garden where you control the door. The sun is bright and warm. The birds are chirping in the trees. A butterfly floats by you. The sound of the water in the fountain fills the air. Are you there?"

She nodded.

"I'm there next to you. In this walled garden nothing can hurt us, disturb us. We are the only two people who exist. You and me."

The sweet seduction of his words painted a picture of them together in her special place. In her mind she reached out and took his hand, finding comfort in his fingers about hers. The connection felt so right. She absorbed his presence, basking in his vitality.

"Continue to breathe deeply in and out. Feel the energy inside you. Focus it in your heart, then unlock it for me."

Ian flattened his hands on her shoulders to further join them. His palms seared into her flesh, centering all her senses on the man who cradled her.

"Expand your heart to allow me inside."

Energy streamed into her, bright and warm, as though the sun rose deep inside her. Her heart unfurled to embrace all parts of her. Nothing mattered but this connection. His power and strength flowed through her. She soared above the walled garden as though she had wings and anything was possible. He was one with her, her heart beating for the both of them.

When he disconnected—a slow severing of their bonds—she floated to the ground, alone now in her special place. Emotions long buried burst forth anew. Their mingled energy, entwined like braids of hair, retracted leaving Anna sated, refreshed—hopeful. The gate in the wall swung open. She could walk through it, safe, her spirit intact.

Slumping forward, she raised her knees and rested her forehead on them. Spent but pleasantly content, she turned her head to slant a look at Ian. "If I didn't know better, I would have thought you were physically a part of me." The second she said it she blushed, realizing the implication of her words. "I mean—"

He pressed his finger over her mouth, humor shining in his eyes. "I know what you meant. And in a manner of speaking I was."

"What do you mean?"

"I connected with you psychically. I felt your worry over your sister, your confusion about what's been happening."

Alarmed that someone might get that close to her emotionally, she said, "Okay, if that's the case, then I think turnabout is fair play. We should do it again. But this time I should be the one in back."

For a second his own alarm flickered in his gaze. Then he veiled it. "I don't think that's possible—"

"Shh." She covered his mouth, determined to see if it were possible. "I want to try. Trust me."

He couldn't deny her challenge if he wanted to continue working with her. He knew he was trapped. With a deep sigh, he nodded. He switched places with her, his back cradled against her front, her legs enclosing him in a soft prison of warm flesh.

When she began reciting the words he'd used, he followed her instruction, his chest expanding with each breath he drew in. He created a special place high on top of the mountain where he grew up and imagined Anna beside him. When he opened himself to her, never expecting her to be successful, her energy nudged his natural barriers, seeking entry. He panicked and closed down. He didn't allow people inside him.

To cover the reason behind the disconnection, he twisted about and drew her into his arms. His mouth came down on hers. For a few seconds, stunned, she did nothing, then she gave in to the sensation he poured into her. Her arms wrapped around his neck, and she held him against her.

He needed to end this before—She nibbled a path to his ear and nipped its lobe. His eyes closed, and he succumbed to her. With a moan, he laid her on the bed and threw his legs over hers, pinning her to the soft mattress while his mouth ravished hers.

Anna never threw herself at a man, but the moment Ian's lips possessed hers, all rational thought fled. She wanted Ian McGregory, felt as though she'd already mated with him on a different level. In his arms she'd come home, and when morning broke she knew that feeling would scare her. But not now. All her senses fixated on him, his mouth devouring hers, his hands skimming over her, fumbling with the buttons on her shirt, the snap on her jeans.

She helped him shed her clothes, then turned her attention to his shirt. Button by slow button she unfastened it, then slipped her palms over the broad expanse of his bare chest. The smooth ripple of his skin beneath her fingertips sent goose bumps up her arms and throughout her body like little electrical currents running between them.

While she explored him, he paid homage to her, taking first one breast then the other into his mouth and sucking on the nipple. When he slid lower, she tensed for a heartbeat, then his tongue delved into her navel before lapping a trail to her womanly core. He tasted her. With a cry she clenched the bedding and urged him to continue.

Releasing her control, she surrendered to the silky feel of his kisses and the rough texture of his fingers as they caressed her. As before when he'd joined her in the walled garden, she soared above, white hot energy flowing through her veins. Another cry split the air as a wave of mind-shattering sensations pushed her over the edge.

Ian moved up her body and positioned himself between her spread legs. With his manhood poised at the threshold of her feminine essence, he framed her face with his hands and stared into her eyes. He invaded her body and thoughts, sending her arching up into him. As he plunged into her again and again, her mind embraced him at the same time she clutched him and screamed her satisfaction.

His roar of release resonated through the room. He collapsed beside her, bringing her up against his length. His harsh breathing matched hers. He searched for her hand and clasped it to his chest. Beneath her fingertips his heart beat rapidly. She smiled, pleased he'd been as affected as she.

"What just happened here?" she finally asked, trying to assimilate all that had transpired. She couldn't. Too many feelings and sensations still gripped her—all things she'd shut down years ago in order to survive.

"Hell if I know. I believe it's called making love."

The wry humor in his words brought her own to the surface. "In certain circles it's called that." Then she remembered how completely she'd felt connected to him and added, "But it was more than that. I can't explain—"

He rolled to his side and stared down at her, tracing the outline of her mouth. "Then don't."

"That tickles."

"You think that does, how about this?" He tickled her side.

She squirmed away, laughing. "Uncle."

"Uncle, so soon? You're not a quitter."

"I know my weak points, so why fight it."

"You have a weak point?" One brow quirked as he lazily stretched out on the bed, his head propped up on the stacked pillows.

She returned to the curve of his arm and rested her head next to his. "Oh, one or two. How about you?"

"I don't have any." He chuckled. "At least none that I will admit."

"Let's see. We could start with too much arrogance, then go on to—"

He twisted toward her, covering her body with his. His mouth came down on hers to stop the flow of words.

"Then go on to stubborn, single-minded," she mumbled against his lips before he pushed his tongue into her mouth.

He pulled back, laughter twinkling in his dark eyes. "I think those words are an apt description of you." He combed her hair back from her face, tenderness in his expression. "I consider both of those qualities a strength. They have come in handy in my job." A shadow clouded his gaze. "Which keeps me from getting sidetracked—at least for any length of time."

"Your job is very important to you."

"It's my life."

The fervent tone of his voice chilled her. She could feel him distancing himself as he straightened to a sitting position, raking his fingers through his hair.

She placed a hand on his back. The muscles beneath

her palm tensed. Life intruded. "You have nothing else?"

He scrambled to his feet and faced her. "My work leaves little time for anything else."

"I sense more behind those words."

He turned away. "I've done more things than most people. I don't regret my life."

"If you say it enough, you might really start believing that."

Stiffening, he threw her a cutting look. "Don't psychoanalyze me. You can't."

"Why? Because you keep yourself locked up?"

Hands clenched at his side, he whirled about. "And you don't?"

"Okay, so we're both alike."

"But I need you to tap into your emotional side."

"Is that all you need—want?" Slipping from the bed, she lifted her chin and met his direct look with one of her own. More than several feet separated them. "For a short time I felt your desire, needs. They were a part of me, and don't deny they weren't. When we made love, it wasn't like anything I've experienced before. It was—" she searched for the right words to describe it, "—all-consuming."

One corner of his mouth curved up. "Thanks. I believe that is a compliment." A gleam entered his eyes.

"Don't you divert the issue here."

He stepped toward her until there were only inches between them. She breathed in the musky scent she would always associate with him. She took a step back. Then another. Suddenly her legs touched the bed.

A full-fledged smile graced his mouth. "I think we should try to repeat that all-consuming experience."

"Just like a man. We get in an argument, and you want to jump to the making up part."

"Who said we were arguing?" He fit a stray strand of

hair behind her ear, then cupped her face. "I can think of better ways to expend my energy."

"I—"

Ian tackled her to the bed, cutting off her flow of words with teasing nibbles. She stopped him and directed his mouth to hers. Her tongue delved inside, her hands holding his head still.

Then he took over, trailing kisses down her body. "Open for me, Anna."

And she did.

Nine

The rays of the moon slanted across Ian's face, drawing his gaze toward the window. He searched the night, probing into the shadows of darkness for any sign of the Chameleon. He felt him. He knew he was watching, but even with his acute eyesight, Ian couldn't see him.

A rustling sound behind him focused his attention on Anna lying on her bed, a sheet only covering the lower part of her body. Sprawled on her stomach, she stretched an arm out toward where he'd been a few moments before, her hand curling about the pillow he'd used.

Her beauty bewitched him. Memories of their mating honed his senses, underscoring how important this woman was to him. He had to protect her. She was too much of a temptation for the Chameleon, and if Ian were truthful with himself, she was too much of a temptation for him. In her embrace there was danger. She stirred emotions in him he'd buried thousands of years before. Only Miranda had come close to opening them up, but in the end he hadn't been able to let go of his defenses, to merge totally with her.

Anna moaned, flipping over, the sheet twisted about her legs. Alarm bolted through him. The look of anguish on her face told him all he needed to know. He rushed to the bed and brought her into his arms, placing his hands on either side of her head.

The Chameleon's projected thoughts whirled through

her. She strained against Ian, trying to push him away. Closing his eyes, he concentrated on what he must do. All his energy tingled through his fingertips and into her. Converging on the Chameleon's message, he met the taunting words with the full force of his power. He swirled around them, again and again, until he enclosed them in a box to protect Anna from them. Her struggles abated. She relaxed in his embrace.

Ian captured the box at the core of his energy, its walls threatening to explode outward, releasing the message into Anna's mind again. He wrestled to contain the Chameleon while withdrawing himself from her thoughts. His strength ebbed. The Chameleon continued to pound at the restriction placed about him. Leaks in his energy peppered Ian's force field. Only a few more seconds. He stiffened his resolve, keeping a firm grip on the box.

Another second passed, and Ian burst from Anna's mind with the box clutched within him. Suddenly the message vanished. He slumped against her, clenching her to his chest. Each breath he drew in singed his lungs. Drained, he pressed Anna into the circle of his arms, worried that the Chameleon would return for another try at her. The searing pain in him subsided, but his body quivered with fatigue. He slid down to lie next to her, still plastered against his length, his embrace like a shield.

***

He raged, smashing his fist into a nearby tree trunk. He couldn't get to her! He could feel the energy emanating from her, and he wanted it—wanted her.

He had no other choice now but to get rid of the Hawk. It wouldn't be easy. It never was when trying to kill one of his own race. And he would have to endure the pain of Hawk's death, as every other Cintarian would.

Different methods of slaying the Hawk played across his mind, but none of them was foolproof. He finally settled on one that gave him a measure of hope. Fading into the alley's inky darkness, he slunk away to make his preparations.

***

A slight pounding in Anna's head pushed her toward wakefulness. She reached up to touch her forehead and encountered her arm trapped beneath an arm. She smiled and cuddled closer to Ian, his male scent enveloping her as completely as his body was. She drank in his familiar aroma and thought of the mountains she had come to associate with him.

He stirred behind her, his hand stroking one of her breasts. "Mmm. This isn't a bad way to wake up," he murmured in her ear before taking a nip of its shell.

She dismissed the nagging ache in her head and concentrated instead on the feel of his fingers as they grazed across her chest, feather soft, leaving a trail of shivers in their wake. "Last night was—" She couldn't finish her sentence because no words would come to mind to describe the life-altering experience she'd had.

"I know. Unbelievable isn't even adequate enough."

She twisted in his arms and leaned back to look into his eyes. "I felt like our joining was more than physical."

"It must be our psychic abilities enhancing our lovemaking."

"That's a possibility." A nervous laugh escaped her lips. "I can't believe I'm calmly lying here talking about psychic abilities. I've never wanted them. They've only brought me trouble in the past."

"But they might be able to help your sister now."

"Yes—if I can learn to tap into them and control them."

"Control comes with practice."

"And you're my teacher."

He planted a kiss on her forehead. "I don't feel like a teacher. Let's call me your guide."

She caressed the darkened skin under his tired eyes. "Did I exhaust you?"

"Nothing I can't handle."

Her hand wandered down his chest until she clasped his manhood. "Now that sounds like a challenge if I ever heard one."

A gleam sparked his eyes. "Are you woman enough to accept?"

"The important question is are you man enough?"

His chuckle danced along her jawline as his lips trailed kisses to her ear. He nibbled on it, whispering, "I'll let you be the judge."

Sensations engulfed her. He stripped away the sheet tangled between them so that only flesh touched flesh. His earthy scent wrapped her in a tight cocoon while the salty taste of his skin glazed her lips as they skimmed over his smooth chest. The rough texture of his day-old beard chafed her neck, making her toes curl.

"Want to go to your walled garden and make love?"

The proposition tantalized her. Was it possible? "How?"

"Through our minds linking."

His suggestion, full of so much intimacy, was irresistible. She nodded against his chest, then with her tongue traced a path to his mouth. "Show me."

He framed her face within his large hands and stared into her eyes. She couldn't see his expression in the dimness, but she felt it go deep to her core, absorbing her essence.

"Anna, think of your garden with its fountain, trees, flowers, lush grass. Now visualize me next to you."

The scent of wildflowers perfumed the air. The warm feel of the sun caressed her skin. The sound of the water bubbling from the fountain enriched the picture in her mind. She stood next to Ian in her walled garden, the lush grass under her bare feet like a carpet of thick velvet, enticing her to lie down on it.

Ian crushed her into his embrace, sweeping her into his arms and gently placing her on the grass. Then he came down to cover her, his hot flesh burning into hers, heating her to a boiling point. The force of his kiss drove her into the cool lushness, a welcomed contrast to their body temperature.

Her sense of rightness heightened when he pulled back and searched her face for a long moment, desire flaring in his eyes. In sweet anticipation her heart thumped madly against her breast, while in the dark reaches of her soul emotions shifted, bloomed. She wanted him as she'd never wanted another man.

She concentrated on the experience of being held by a man who could arouse her with just a touch or a look. Running her hand down his roughened jawline, she relished the gritty feel beneath her fingertips that somehow accentuated his strength. She didn't stop there but continued downward to caress the dusting of dark hair covering his muscular chest.

When she began to glide her hands even lower, he dragged them away, securing them over her head. "I want us to savor and remember every second of our joining. If you touch me there, I'll—"

She smiled. "Lose control? Would that be so bad?"

He didn't answer her. Instead, he thrust his tongue between her lips, tasting his own salt on them. He couldn't lose control, but his carefully constructed walls were crumbling each second he held Anna to his pounding heart. Something about her spoke to a part of him he'd denied for so long. He frantically tried to repair his fragile composure, but her passionate moan echoed in his ears, sending him over the edge.

For a few seconds he merged with her, giving her a

glimpse of the person he was under all the layers of disguise. He let her see the loneliness he usually held at bay, the restlessness no one else saw.

In turn he experienced the pain of her childhood, the struggle to create an identity that denied her true abilities, her love of teaching, the deep sadness tangled up with her feelings toward her sister. The connection was fleeting, but the sense of completeness he felt surprised him. When it was severed, a yearning pierced his armor. He wanted her again and again as he'd never wanted another woman.

***

Terri rose when Anna entered the hospital room with Ian right behind her. "You're early today."

"I have to meet with some students before class, so we decided to come now. How's Sandra doing?" Anna asked, knowing the answer before Terri said anything.

"The same."

"Has she had any visitors?" Ian came to stand beside Anna, asking the same question he did every day.

"Someone who worked with her at the library. Betsy Mayo?"

"Yes, they both worked in the research department." Anna stared at her younger sister and wondered if she would ever be able to tell her she loved her. Now she regretted all the times she hadn't said anything, had let their differences concerning their psychic abilities stand between them.

"That young man hasn't returned?"

Ian's question reminded Anna yet again the danger her sister might still be in. Goose bumps pebbled her skin.

"Not since that first night. I'll let you know immediately if he does."

"You think he might have something to do with this?" Anna asked, chafing her hands up and down her arms.

"I'm not ruling out anyone. I want to know about his

relationship with Sandra, and they obviously had a relationship of some sort because of his comment that night."

"She helped a lot of graduate students with their research. That may be all it is."

"Possibly, but I—" The door opening halted his next words.

Dr. Nelson entered, smiling when he saw Anna. "I'm glad you're here. I was going to call you later, but this is better. I hate talking on the phone about a patient's situation."

"What's wrong?" Tension whipped down Anna's length. She moved to her sister's side and took her hand. "She looks the same."

"She is. But by the end of the week if there hasn't been a change, we'll have to move her to a long-term care facility."

"Move her?" Anna squeezed her sister's hand, wishing she could get her to wake up.

"Insurance reasons. And really there's nothing more we can do for her here. It's in God's hands now. We have a good long-term care facility connected with the hospital. Before you go today, stop by the nurses' station and pick up a brochure." Dr. Nelson walked to the same side as Anna and checked Sandra briefly before continuing on his rounds.

Anna sank down onto the chair next to the bed, still holding her sister's hand. "She isn't going to get better."

"He didn't say that." Ian clasped her shoulder, his fingers warm, comforting.

"He doesn't have to. I could see it in his eyes."

"We have to hope she'll wake up."

The fervent tone in Ian's voice conveyed his own frustrations. Sandra was the key to his investigation. But none of the others had woken up. Anna cradled Sandra's cold hand between hers, desperate to transmit life and warmth into her sister. *Please, Sandra, don't die. I have so much to tell you. To make up for. Give me that chance.* Suddenly a feeling of love and forgiveness tingled through her. She snapped her head around to look at Sandra's face, feeling as though she would be staring back at her. Her sister's eyes were still closed, but the tingling sensation continued. More emotions flooded Anna. Fear. Betrayal.

"Who was it Sandra? Who did this to you?"

A friend.

Anna gripped her sister's hand tighter. "Who?"

Her question met silence. The coldness of Sandra's fingers amplified the sudden break in their connection. Deflated, Anna sagged forward, wanting to scream her frustration. Doubts about her talent plagued her as she finally lifted her head and glanced at Ian. She released her connection with Sandra and stood, facing him. "I get the feeling the person was a friend, but then I already thought he was since she went to bed—" The words clogged her throat. Tears jammed against them. "This isn't working. I know she felt fear and betrayal and that he was a friend, but we already knew that. My sister is very particular about the men she dates—dated."

"Sometimes you can't push it. I don't want you to give up. He's still out there, and Sandra is still our only witness." Ian stepped forward to draw her into his embrace.

Upset, confused, and restless, Anna shrugged away. Raking her hand through her hair, she headed for the door. "I'll be at the nurses' station."

Ian started to follow her. Terri stopped him.

"Give her some time alone. Besides, you and I need to talk."

"Is there something you didn't want to say in front of

Anna? Was there someone else here?"

"No, but I don't want to say this in front of her. Be careful. Getting too involved with a human is costly. Remember Melinda and what happened there."

Cold reality slapped him in the face. He frowned, memories of the night spent with Anna swamping him. Their making love was a mistake—one he couldn't repeat. "I don't have to be reminded of Melinda. Even after hundreds of years the pain is still with me."

"That's why we can't become too tangled in a person's life. It's such a fleeting time we can have with them."

"I know. We discovered long ago it was best to remain apart emotionally."

"But?"

"But it may be too late."

"You have more control than most."

"But I'm only—" one side of his mouth lifted in a mocking grin, "I guess I can't say human. But I do have weaknesses like everyone else."

"And Anna is one of them?"

"I don't know. I do know she is special. She has a great talent, which means she has a lot of Cintarian in her."

Terri's eyes narrowed, her brow creased. "But we can't acknowledge any human/Cintarian mix. Too risky."

"It has been done."

"A few times. The last one over seven hundred years ago."

"Times are changing. The human race is looking to outer space now. Maybe this is a time to rethink our position."

She gasped. "I can't believe I'm hearing you say that. You have protected us from exposure for over a thousand years. Your own father died protecting our secret."

He drew up straight. "And I will do the same. You

needn't worry about me, Terri. Now, I'd better go get Anna before she decides to leave without me."

Ian left the room and walked toward the nurses' station. Anna stood reading a brochure, a tiny frown on her brow, her lips puckered. The sight of them caused the memories of the night before to resurface. Something he didn't want to acknowledge festered deep inside him. He cared what happened to her. Her safety was paramount to him—and not because she could help him find the Chameleon. No, he was afraid it went much deeper than that.

***

Anna handed the phone to Ian. "It's for you. Terri."

He snatched it from her grasp, cupping his palm over the receiver. "We'll talk about this later." Then to Terri he asked, "What's up?"

His grip tightened, a scowl descending over his features. "Are you sure?" He wrote something on the note pad next to the phone. "Okay, I'll check it out."

Anna spun away from Ian and paced the living room. The moment she heard him put the receiver down she tensed. She stopped behind the recliner and clutched its brown leather cushion. "I know this is serious, Ian, but I can't have you following me everywhere. I feel like I'm the one in prison here. Today in class all I could think about was you watching me while I lectured. I'm never self-conscious. I was today."

"What do you suggest I do? Let the man come after you?"

Her fingernails dug into the cool leather. "Maybe you should. I don't know if I can ever give you the information you want, and frankly the doctor isn't too optimistic about Sandra recovering. How else can we get this man? Let's set a trap for him."

A thunderous expression chased away his scowl, slanting his black brows down and carving deep lines into his face. "No!"

"We are partners. I do have a say in things."

"Not on my watch."

The urge to stamp her foot swept over her, but she remained still and continued to clench the leather. "What if he moves on when he finds he can't get to me? Then he's gone, and more women will die because we couldn't catch him." Her voice cracked. "I can't connect enough with Sandra." She buried her face in her hands. "I can't believe the one time I want to use my talent, it's not working well enough."

"I'm pushing you too hard." His hand touched her shoulder, and she went into his embrace.

"I'm letting my sister down. Maybe we should go back to her apartment."

"We can try it later. Right now I'm going to check out this address. The unknown young man who visited Sandra came back, and this time she found out who he was."

"Who?"

"Rob Alexander. I have his address." Ian showed her the piece of paper.

"That's out a ways from Lexington. I'll come with you. I might recognize him."

"No. If he is the killer, I don't want you around."

"But—"

He covered her mouth with his fingers. "No arguments. I couldn't do my job if you're there. I'd worry too much about you."

"I know how to get out of the way," she protested.

He framed her face and stared long and hard into her eyes. "Look. I'll sit outside your classroom when you're lecturing. I'll try to back off some. But under no circumstances will I use you as bait or put you in danger if I can help it." He kissed the tip of her nose. "Let's go."

"I thought I wasn't going with you?"

"You aren't. I'm taking you to Terri. You can sit with her and Sandra until I get back. With any luck this may be the break we need. If Rob Alexander isn't the man maybe he knows the man who took his place in your sister's life."

"I don't know who Rob Alexander is." She took a deep sigh. "I don't know very much about my sister's life since we left home. We both live in the same town—work for the same university. That doesn't say much about our relationship."

When she started for the door, Ian grabbed her arm and swung her around to face him. "Anna, a relationship works both ways. Don't beat yourself up over the past. It'll only get in the way of you helping Sandra now."

One corner of her mouth tilted upward. "I guess when you're guilt ridden it's hard to be worry-free."

"After I see this Rob guy, we'll talk some more about this."

But as Anna walked to the car, she felt all talked out. She kept seeing the mysterious man in her mind, but he was surrounded by heavy fog, his features blank. She could almost reach out and touch him, but a few inches separated them, and she couldn't move to close the gap no matter how hard she tried. Frustration churned her stomach into a huge snarl on the short drive to the hospital.

When Ian pulled up to the entrance, he said, "Go straight up to Sandra's room and stay there until I pick you up."

"Aye, aye, captain." She saluted him.

He frowned. "Promise?"

She climbed out of the car and leaned down. "Yes, I'll be a good girl."

He grumbled something that she was just as glad not to have heard and waved her toward the sliding double doors. She hurried inside and noticed he didn't leave until she was in the building.

When she entered her sister's room, Terri looked up, puzzled. "I didn't expect you back today."

Anna walked to the chair beside Sandra's bed and sat. "What else was Ian going to do with me since he had to check that man out?"

"What man?"

Anna's gaze riveted to Terri sitting on the couch by the window. "The one you called about?"

"I haven't talked to Ian since you two left earlier today."

Ten

"But you called him not thirty minutes ago and gave him the name and address of that young man who visited Sandra." Slowly Anna rose, her legs quivering. "I heard you!"

Terri shook her head. "It wasn't me. What happened?"

"A person who sounded exactly like you—and claimed to be you—called and told Ian that Rob Alexander had been to see Sandra again. You—I mean that person—gave Ian Rob's home address. That's where Ian is going." With each word of explanation she spoke, dread encompassed Anna, until her whole body trembled. "It's a trap. Does Ian have a cell phone?"

"No, he doesn't like them and will only carry one when he absolutely has to."

Anna swore. "I need to warn him."

"You shouldn't leave here. I'll go."

"No. I can't protect Sandra if the killer is trying to lure us away from her, but I can warn Ian. I'll be safe with him. Can I borrow your keys? Ian's only got a ten minute head start. I may be able to take a shortcut."

"I don't know, Anna. I—"

Anna held out her hand. "We're wasting time."

Frowning, Terri dug into her purse and withdrew her keys. "Ian won't be happy with me letting you leave my protection."

"If Ian's hurt or worse, he can't track anyone down.

Where's your car?"

"The south parking lot, fifth row from the door. It's a new red Mustang."

Snatching the keys from Terri, Anna raced for the elevator.

It couldn't come fast enough. She watched the numbers change as it rose to her floor, but it seemed like an eternity before the doors opened. On the ride down to the ground level, Anna's heart hammered so loud and quick she was sure the other riders could hear it. She forced herself to take deep, even breaths. She wouldn't be any good to Ian if she collapsed or had a wreck before she could get to him.

Outside, the air cooled her heated cheeks as she scanned the large lot for Terri's red car. When she saw it, she ran toward it, a black truck backing out of its space nearly mowing her down. She skidded to a halt, endured the man's obscene gesture and waited until he pulled completely out of his parking space. Then she hurried forward, more cautiously this time.

In Terri's Mustang she glanced at the clock and swore. Time was against her. Screeching from the south lot, she pushed down on the accelerator as much as she dared. Her grip on the steering wheel sent pain up her arm, but she couldn't relax. Fear had as firm a grip on her as she did on the wheel. Visions of her and Ian in her garden making love filled her thoughts. They had shared something beautiful. She couldn't lose him now.

***

Ian pulled up in front of the small, red-brick house in an older neighborhood. Looking up and down the deserted street, he switched off the engine and sat, studying the area. With his mind he reached out and probed the dwelling. He couldn't feel anyone's presence inside. Perfect. That gave him time to look around before confronting Rob Alexander.

Climbing from the car, he headed for the back yard. He'd rather break in without the neighbors' prying eyes. Maneuvering around a turned over trash can with garbage scattered on the ground, he opened the iron gate, wincing when he heard its creaking sound. He kept his mind focused outward for any signs of trouble and hurried to the door.

After jimmying the lock, he slipped inside. Immediately the sense of danger drummed against him. He moved quickly through the kitchen and into the living room. He pushed his mind to the farthest reaches of the house.

No one lived here!

The hairs on the nape of his neck rose. The doors of the snare banged shut. Ian dove for the front door.

***

When Anna turned onto the street, she saw her car parked three houses away. Too far, she screamed silently as she pressed her foot on the accelerator, then stomped it down on the brake a few seconds later, behind her vehicle.

The pounding of her heart matched the pounding of her feet as she raced toward the house. Ten yards away. Five.

The front door opened.

She started to shout Ian's name.

Boom!

The force of the blast drove her back. She slammed into the sidewalk, rolled over and covered her head. Her ears rang. The ground shook. Pieces of debris pelted her. Shards of glass cut into her flesh as though she were tangled in a hedge of thorns. Searing heat singed her, propelling her toward the street. A sulfureous odor assailed her. She clasped a hand over her mouth and nose and crawled toward the curb. Sharp glass and bits of metal and wood littered the ground, slicing into her palm and knees. She blocked the pain and kept inching forward, her whole body trembling.

Another blast reverberated through her numb mind.

Ian!

She made it to the street and collapsed, then drew herself up into a ball and tried to still the tremors that shook her as surely as the explosion shook the earth beneath her.

She looked toward the flames consuming the house. Her eyes stung. A continuous ringing sound resonated in her head. She thought of Ian trapped inside—dead.

I was too late.

Tears flooded her eyes and rolled down her cheeks. Through the blur she saw him, lying on the ground. The sight of his still body, completely intact, sent her to her feet. She swayed and nearly dropped back to the curb.

Closing her eyes, she drew on what strength she had left. She crept toward Ian, her body refusing to function properly. She had to pull him to safety. Pain laced each movement, but she made herself concentrate on moving forward.

Kneeling next to Ian, she felt for a pulse. Relief trembled through her when she found a faint one. Glancing around her, she saw a few people coming out of their houses, their stunned faces intent on the house going up in flames.

The nearest person was a woman in her seventies who could barely walk. No help there. A young man at the end of the street approached slowly, as though he couldn't believe what had just happened. She was the only one who could help Ian.

Fearing another explosion, she had to move him. With all the energy she could muster she slid her arms under his chest and dragged him toward the street.

The sound of sirens battered at her fragile composure. Straining, her breathing labored, she made it to the street with Ian. Once at a relatively safe distance, she stopped and gently released him. Amazed that he'd made it out of the house in one piece, she checked his pulse again, praying he was still alive.

Surprised that his life forces were beating stronger, she began to assess his injuries. He was covered with scratches and cuts. Blood from a gash matted his hair. His torn, dirty clothes hung in shreds off his body.

He groaned and stirred.

The blare of the sirens grew nearer. Anna spotted a fire truck barreling around the corner, another following.

Ian raised his hand to his head. Rolling to his side, he felt the gash above his forehead. His eyes slowly opened. He tried to grin, but it faded instantly.

With a wince he struggled to a sitting position. "What are you doing here?"

"What are you doing trying to sit up?" She supported his back, running her hands up and down him, needing to reassure herself that he would be all right.

"It was a setup."

"I know. Terri didn't call. That's why I'm here. To warn you. Next time carry a cell phone."

This time his grin stayed a few seconds. "I might just have to take up the habit of being instantly available to anyone."

The paramedics arrived. Ian shot her a look that silenced any words. He allowed one to check him over while the other assessed Anna. Except for some cuts and bruises which the paramedic cleaned, she was all right. As soon as she was patched up, she headed back to Ian.

"Sir, we need to transport you to the hospital."

Ian shook the man's hand off his arm. "No. No hospitals. I'll be fine."

"You've got a sprained ankle, several broken ribs, and you may have internal bleeding."

"No." Ian pushed himself to his feet and wobbled.

Anna clasped him, letting him lean into her. "Ian, please listen to the man."

"I will be fine," he said through clenched teeth. Pain marked the lines deeply into his face.

A grimace and stern determination greeted her inspection. She turned to the paramedic. "If he has any trouble, I'll get him to the hospital."

"Lady, I don't recommend him leaving without seeing a doctor."

"I'll see my own doctor. Don't worry." Ian placed his hand on Anna's shoulder, his body pressed up against her side.

She staggered momentarily under his weight, but steadied herself and wound her arm around his waist. Her own minor wounds throbbed. She wanted to shake some sense into him, but somehow knew it wouldn't do any good. Short of losing consciousness, he would not go to the hospital.

The paramedic positioned himself on Ian's other side and helped Anna get him to Terri's car. After brushing the windshield's shattered glass off the seat, she assisted him into the Mustang, smiled her thanks to the paramedic, clasped Ian's seat belt over him, then straightened. A police car screeched to a halt a few feet from her. She glanced down at Ian who had his head resting back on the seat. Shutting the door, she met the police on the driver's side of the car.

"What happened here?" He took out his note pad.

"I'm not sure. My friend was on the porch when the house blew up."

The policeman bent down and looked at Ian. "And he's alive?"

"Yes, thankfully," she breathed the words, still amazed. "I'm taking him to see a doctor." She hoped to convince him to see one.

"Give me your names and addresses so I can take a formal statement later."

Anna supplied the policeman with the necessary information, then cleaned the glass from her seat and slipped behind the steering wheel. She peered at Ian. A pallor cast his features in white.

As she started the car, he murmured, "You are not taking me to see a doctor. I just need to rest. I'll be fine tomorrow morning."

"With broken ribs and no telling what else?"

"The paramedic was wrong."

"Since when did you become a doctor?" She pulled away from the burning house, shivering at the sight of flames and smoke filling the sky.

"I know my own body. Just take me to your house."

"You've got to be the most stubborn man I've ever met," she mumbled as she drove away, the flashing red lights in the rearview mirror underscoring the danger they were in.

***

Anna finally closed the door, leaving Ian alone in her bedroom. He shifted, trying to make himself more comfortable, but his injuries were far worse than the paramedic had said. At times like these he sympathized with humans. Pain pierced every part of his body, as though tiny knives were continually stabbing him. It had taken all his strength and willpower not to succumb to it in front of Anna or the people at the scene of the explosion.

He needed time. Time to heal.

Then he needed Anna. To fortify his life forces. He didn't want to use her like that, but he had to recover as quickly as possible. The Chameleon was stepping up his activities. The threat to his race—to Anna—was great.

His eyes slid closed. He drew in on himself, every bodily function slowing down as he concentrated on mending his injuries.

***

Sitting at the table, he took a sip of his drink while listening to the others talk around him. He would have known if Ian McGregory had died in the explosion, blown to tiny bits. He would have felt a part of his inner self ripped away. But there had been nothing.

The Hawk had survived his trap. Rage simmered below his calm facade. His tight grip on his glass conveyed the increasing difficulty he had in controlling his anger. Now he had to come up with another plan, for he would have Anna. The Hawk's interest in her went beyond his duty to the Cintarians. More than anything, he wanted to take something else away from the Hawk.

***

Anna eased the door open, peering into her darkened bedroom. The light from the wall slanted across the bed, revealing Ian stretched out on top of the covers, perfectly still, his chest not even rising and falling. Alarm bolted through her. She should have checked on him earlier, she thought as she hurried to him.

The quivering in her fingers as she pressed them to his neck amplified her fear that she shouldn't have listened to him about leaving him alone. Why hadn't she done what she knew was best—take him to the hospital?

For a few seconds she couldn't find a pulse. Her anxiety multiplied. She reached for the phone on the bedside table. A hand clamped about her arm, halting her action.

"Don't, Anna. I'm fine. I told you I would be."

Relieved to hear the strong thread in his voice, she sank down onto the bed next to him and searched his face in the dim light from the hallway. "I thought you'd lost consciousness, or worse—" she swallowed hard, "— died."

One corner of his mouth tilted up. "You can't get rid of me that easily."

"Don't joke, Ian. You were set up."

"Which means that I'm getting close. What we're doing must be right."

"The next time he might succeed—"

"Anna, don't think about that. There won't be a next time."

She sighed. "You don't know that unless one of your talents is reading the future."

"No, but I know I will be fine."

The strong conviction in his voice should have reassured her. It didn't. She could still remember seeing him at the front door, then all hell had broken loose. The next few minutes after that everything had been hazy. She wasn't even sure how he ended up lying on the lawn.

She started to rise. "I'll leave you to get some more rest."

He stopped her with a firm grip on her hand. "No, stay with me."

His husky appeal surprised her. She saw the way he'd looked after the explosion, and yet now he was acting as though it were nothing but a minor accident. She hesitated, wondering if he was delirious.

"I need you, Anna."

"But what about your injuries?"

"I told you I wasn't hurt that badly." He pushed himself up onto his elbows, then scooted over so she could lie next to him.

This wasn't a good idea. Her own minor injuries hurt, so she could imagine what his felt like. Why was he pretending he was all right? He couldn't be. Confusion held her poised at the side of the bed.

"Let me hold you while you sleep."

The seduction in his voice melted her resistance. After switching off the hall light, she slipped into bed with him. He drew her close.

"I wish I could do more, but to tell you the truth, it's kind of been a rough day," he murmured against the top of her head.

"No? For a minute there I thought Superman didn't have any faults."

He stiffened. "I'm no Superman."

"I was just teasing," she said in response to his serious tone.

"Rest, Anna. I'll make sure nothing disturbs you while you sleep."

Amazed that even while hurting he insisted on protecting her, she said, "I do know how to take care of myself. I've been doing it for years."

A faint chuckle tickled the top of her head. "Then humor me."

"Okay, but don't get the idea that I'll do everything you say."

"No, never."

"If you weren't hurting so much, I'd punch you in the stomach for that smart remark."

"Ouch."

She peered at him. "I didn't do anything."

"The mere thought made me tense. That hurt."

"You see. You should have had a doctor look at you."

"Tell you what, Anna. If tomorrow morning I'm not better, you can have your way with me. No protest."

She tried to read his expression, but the dark hid it. "I will remind you of that tomorrow morning." She settled back alongside him, enjoying the warmth from his body, his musky male scent that always made her feel safe. "Ian?

Do you think there really is a Rob Alexander?"

He enfolded her in his arms. "That's the first thing I'm going to check into tomorrow. Now, if you don't let me rest, I'm taking back my promise."

The exhaustion that crept into his voice prompted her to say, "I can check tomorrow after I take you to see the doctor." She couldn't see how he could be much better after what he'd gone through. But for the time being she would humor him.

"Shh, Anna." Ian grasped her head and pressed it to his chest, even though pain slashed into him.

She relaxed against him finally, her breathing deep and even. When she slipped into the realm of dreams, he gathered his deteriorating energy. With his hands cradling her face, he flowed into her mind, siphoning some of her life forces to help mend his. Careful not to take too much, he left quickly before she realized anything was amiss.

He lay still, feeling the gentle rise and fall of her chest against him. He hoped what energy he took was all he would need. But if he had to, he would feed again before morning.

***

Ian filled Anna's dreams as though he'd come into her mind and become a part of them. As they faded, the lingering feeling that he had possessed her stayed in her thoughts while sunlight danced across her face. His warmth invaded her consciousness. His scent overwhelmed her senses.

"Good morning, Anna."

His whispered words against her ear bathed it in tantalizing sensations. *Am I still dreaming?*

The comforting world of dreams drew her back. Exhaustion clung to every part of her, and she didn't want to wake up.

"We have a lot to do today. And if you don't get up

soon, you'll be late for your first class."

Ian sounded way too cheerful, as though nothing unusual had happened the day before. Snuggling closer to his warmth, she fought the ties of weariness that held her down.

"As much as I would love to stay in bed all day, I can't and neither can you."

A brief kiss on her lips caused her to ease one eye open. She stared at Ian looming over her. A grin sparkled his dark eyes like the night caught in the first rays of the morning sun. Both eyes popped open when she noticed there wasn't a scratch or cut on his face. She immediately looked up to where his gash was. A thin red line was the only indication he'd even had a deep cut.

"What happened? Did I sleep a week? What day is it?" She scrambled into a sitting position to assess the rest of him.

"I told you I heal fast."

She ran her hand over his chest, only a few faint bruises on it. She examined his sprained ankle, swollen the night before, perfectly normal this morning. "No one heals this fast. Who are you?"

Eleven

"You know who I am." Ian stretched as if testing his body to make sure it worked perfectly.

Anna gestured toward her scratches and cuts, visible even in her long T-shirt. "Don't play games with me. This is what a person should look like—or worse—after being in an explosion."

Running his finger over several of her abrasions, he frowned. "You could have been hurt seriously. You should have stayed with Terri."

She batted his hand away and put the width of the bed between them. "Don't change the subject. We're talking about you."

"Boring subject. You're much more interesting." He gave her a lopsided grin as he sat up, again stretching.

For a moment her attention strayed to the broad expanse of his chest, to his firm, muscled legs, to the fact he was only dressed in his boxers. Intimate thoughts leaped into her mind. She wanted to caress that chest, those legs. She wanted to remove his boxers and—No! She needed answers!

"Ian, if that is even your name, I want to know how you could recover so quickly. You had some serious injuries. Any normal person would have been in the hospital. I thought I would be taking you this morning, in fact. So, I want some answers and now. Who are you?"

His brows drew together, and his eyes narrowed. "I

don't know what you want me to tell you. I am Ian McGregory. I work for the FBI."

She glared at him. "And?"

"I've always healed fast. A doctor once told me that it has something to do with my genes. I don't have any other explanation. This is how I've always been." Ian spread his arms wide, lifting his shoulders in a shrug. "What else can I say?"

She scrambled from the bed, her hands fisted at her sides. Exhaustion cleaved to every part of her, but she was determined to face him with her suspicions that something wasn't right. "I don't know. This seems so impossible."

"Well, I suppose another explanation could be that I'm an alien bent on taking over the world." He screwed his face into a menacing look before his expression dissolved into a teasing grin.

"That's impossible, too."

"So, I'm a freak."

She flinched at the word. Dragging deep breaths into her lungs, she wrestled to make sense of the situation. Her gaze skimmed over him again, taking in the few remaining signs that even indicated he'd recently been in an explosion. The almost healed gash on his forehead and the slight discoloration along his ribcage unnerved her more than she thought possible. Her faith wavered, and she began to wonder if she could trust him.

Nothing was as it seemed.

He started around the bed toward her. She moved away, her legs trembling as though she'd run up a twenty story flight of steps. She needed to sit down. The chair was across the room, and the bed wasn't a good idea. Her back came into contact with the dresser. He kept advancing. Her gaze darted about, trying to find a way to escape. She sidled toward the door.

Ian blocked her exit. His hands gripped her arms and hauled her up against him. "I can't explain it, Anna. That's the way I am. I've always been different. I guess that's why I could identify with you."

The vulnerability that edged his voice tore at her heart. She knew exactly what it was like to be different from everyone else. But still, this seemed so impossible. Confusion and weariness weighed her down. She blinked, really wanting to close her eyes and lie down and sleep some more. She had so many things she should say, but she murmured, "I need to sit down."

Something flashed into his dark eyes. He immediately gathered her to him and helped her toward the bed.

"No, the chair," she managed to say before closing her eyes and allowing him to lead her to it.

He knelt in front of her. "Do you want me to call the university and cancel your classes?"

She shook her head, then rested it on the back cushion. "Give me another thirty minutes to rest. I should be better by then. I just think everything is catching up with me. These past few weeks haven't been what I would call typical."

"Sure. Can I get you something? Coffee? Aspirin?"

"Yeah, your genes. I wouldn't mind bouncing back like you."

Silence greeted her gibe. Anna eased an eye open. Ian hovered over her, a frown carved into his dark features.

"I will take some coffee. I'll be in the kitchen after I take a shower."

He didn't budge.

"Go. I'm fine. Tired, but this certainly isn't the first time I've felt this way."

For a long moment his gaze traveled over her, as though he didn't believe she was all right. When he reestablished eye contact, she saw worry and something else in his expression. Guilt? She supposed he blamed himself for her injuries of the day before.

"Ian, even knowing what I do, I would have still come to the house to warn you."

"If you'd been any closer—"

"But I wasn't. You know, if you don't get me that coffee, I'll never awake up."

He left her sitting in the overstuffed chair with her eyes closed and her body stretched out as if she'd collapsed into it like a rag doll. The sight hammered at his conscience, heightening his guilt. He'd taken some of her energy to heal his body. He knew she would feel lethargic for a good part of the day but be fine by the evening. Still, his need bothered him. She was stronger than most. The sweet taste of her essence had been extraordinary.

***

Anna watched the nurse and orderly settle her sister into her new room at the long-term care facility. After hooking up her IV and monitor, they left. Anna leaned against the pale green painted wall and stared at Sandra lying in the hospital bed, features almost as pale as the white sheets surrounding her.

A lump clogged Anna's throat. She swallowed several times, but couldn't contain the emotions swelling up inside her. "I'd like to visit with my sister—alone," she said to Terri and Ian.

Terri glanced at Ian, then replied, "Sure. We'll be right outside the door if you need us."

Anna waited until they'd left before taking the chair next to the bed and pulling it closer. She had to talk to someone about the bewilderment she felt, about her doubts. At least this morning she was more rested. The day before had passed in a blur. She'd gone to her classes, but she wasn't sure she had made any sense to her students. After that she'd come home and collapsed, sleeping from the late afternoon until four in the morning. When she'd awakened, Ian lay next to her, one leg and arm thrown loosely over her. She'd slid out from beneath him and sat in the chair, watching him sleep, trying to dismiss the apprehension nibbling at her belief in him.

Grasping her sister's hand, Anna cradled it between hers. "I don't know what to believe anymore, Sandra. Some pretty strange things have been happening lately, and I can't explain them. You know me. There's always a logical explanation. Well, I don't have one for this. Ian healed overnight from some serious injuries. I've never heard of that."

She glanced back at the closed door and lowered her voice. "I'm not a doctor, but that seems impossible. He says it's in his genes. Then again what other explanation could it be? First, you end up in the hospital in a deep coma the doctors can't explain. Second, my psychic abilities are going haywire. Third, Ian McGregory. At times I feel like he's inside of me. He says he's psychic, too. And I suppose that's it, but—"

Anna couldn't finish the thought. Confusion reigned in her mind. She wanted her old life back. She wanted her sister well. She wanted to believe in Ian.

***

"Okay, tell me what happened at the house." Terri spun toward Ian, her hands balled on her hips, her features pinched into a frown.

"It was a setup. There is a Rob Alexander, and as soon as I get a picture of him, I'll show it to you. I bet he's the one who came to the hospital that evening, but I don't think he's the Chameleon. Too easy."

"That means the Chameleon knows about him. How?"

"Sandra told him?"

"Interesting." Her expression relaxed into a neutral facade. "Do you think Rob and Sandra were dating before the Chameleon came into her life?"

"That's where Anna and I are going when we leave here. I'm going to have a little chat with this Rob Alexander. Just maybe, if the Chameleon knows about him, Rob will know who the Chameleon is."

"As you said, too easy."

Ian grinned. "I know, but every once in a while I like to hope."

"If he's the same one, he was an angry young man. Even though you have my description, get a picture. I'd like to ID him for sure." Terri leaned back against the wall and crossed her arms over her chest. "The Chameleon might move on since you've proved indestructible."

"There's a part of me that wishes he does, but there's a part of me that doesn't. I'm so close. I don't want to start over in another location. And we both know he won't stop. He's accelerating. Once a Cintarian gives in to the lure to totally possess a human, he doesn't stop voluntarily."

"And the Chameleon has a score to settle with you. You brought in his father and older brother. All of this started with his brother's recent death."

Those long-ago memories assailed Ian, causing him to suck in a deep, bracing breath that did nothing to relieve the pressure in his chest. He'd been the one to find his father's broken, crushed body after the Chameleon's sire had killed him. Ian's jaw clamped down so tightly that pain shot down his neck. Once he'd hunted down the Chameleon's father, his older brother took up where their father had left off—and now it had started all over again with the Chameleon.

"Sometimes I think this whole affair with the Chameleon is for my benefit. He loves to taunt me. He always has, for hundreds of years. Thankfully only until recently involving the humans." He clenched his hands, wishing he could ram them through the wall. "I'm responsible for those women dying. I'm responsible for Sandra lying in that room. If Anna ever truly found out about—"

Terri gripped his arm, thrusting her face into his. "Don't go there, Ian. The Chameleon's responsible, and you know that. You don't usually allow guilt to take hold. Why now?"

He wrenched free of her hold and stepped back. "Because I used Anna the night before last. I needed her energy to heal, and I took it."

"Ah, now I understand. We have to do that sometimes. She's recovered and is fine. You might not have recovered without using her." Terri covered the space between them. This time she settled her hand on his shoulder and kneaded her fingers into his taut muscles. "If you'd been able to ask her, she would have gladly done it for you. I've seen how she looks at you. She cares."

"Which makes it worse. I wanted to ask. I almost did."

"You can't! You can't break our prime law."

"Don't you think I know that better than anyone?" He plunged his hand through his hair, over and over. Frustration churned deep inside him.

"You did more than recover your energy. You mated with her. I thought you didn't want to get involved."

"I didn't. I don't." The frustration coursing through his body hardened his words.

"You care."

"More than I should. After Miranda, I won't watch another human I love die. I won't live a lie. I nearly—" He couldn't finish the sentence. The memory of holding Miranda in his arms when she took her last breath overpowered him as if it were occurring right then. Damn, he wouldn't allow his emotions to trap him again. That was why his race had learned long ago to bury them.

"You need to return to the Mountain."

"I will—after I catch the Chameleon. I'll have to take him home to face the Circle."

"Then you'll be able to reconnect with our people. Being out in this world too long can dissociate us from our race and what it means to be a Cintarian. You need to return home as soon as possible."

He laughed, a bitter twist to the sound. "Home! That's millions of miles away. It died thousands of years ago."

"You know what I mean. Quit being difficult. Earth is our home now and has been most of our lifetime."

"But I remember Cintar. We could be ourselves and live openly, as we are supposed to." He realized as long as he lived in the human's world, his life was a lie, his true self restrained in a prison with invisible walls. That knowledge pierced the barrier he kept around his emotions. He envied the humans the ability to live as they truly were.

"I was a child when we had to flee. Have you ever wondered what happened to the others?"

The door opening prevented Ian from answering. He pressed his lips together and watched Anna emerge from her sister's room. The dark circles under her eyes attested to the toll Sandra's ordeal was having on her, but what tugged at him was the shadow of doubt in her gaze when she looked at him. She knew something wasn't right. He could feel her pulling back, and he knew he shouldn't do anything to stop that. But he wanted to.

"I'm ready to go see Rob Alexander," she said, her gaze sliding away from him.

He hoped that at least he could give Anna her sister back before he left. Then maybe he could forgive himself for his lack of control, for sharing more of himself than he should have. What if she was with child? The possibility elated and frightened him at the same time.

***

Anna trudged up the third flight of stairs, following Ian to apartment 3B. The scuff marks along the baseboard and the dingy gray tint to the walls accentuated the building's disarray. Musky odors, like ripe socks left damp in the bottom of a pile of dirty clothes and food fried in old grease, assaulted her. She sneezed. Ian glanced back at her and offered a smile of apology before rapping on the door to 3B.

For a long moment no one answered. Ian knocked again, louder. "He's home."

Anna shivered. "You call this home?"

The door creaked open a crack. "What do you want?"

"I need to speak with Rob Alexander." Ian showed the man his FBI badge.

"What about?"

"Are you Rob Alexander?"

Anna peered into the small gap. One large blue eye peered back.

"I'm busy. Come back another time."

With lightning speed Ian shoved open the door, propelling the tall, muscular man back into his apartment. He stumbled, caught himself and straightened. His glare cut into Ian as the FBI agent moved inside and kicked the door closed.

"You can't come in here. Do you have a warrant?" The man's gaze flicked between Ian and Anna.

"Is there a reason I should get one?"

The man started to take a step back, stopped, and squared his shoulders. "No, of course not. What do you want?"

"Are you Rob Alexander?"

"Yes."

"I want to talk to you about Sandra Stanfield."

"Who?"

"The woman you visited in the hospital a few days ago."

The harshness in Ian's voice froze Anna. His demeanor spoke of a man very capable of taking care of himself and protecting anyone in his safekeeping. Rob Alexander obviously sensed this. His attention darted to the door, as if he were a ferret calculating a plan of escape. But Ian was even taller and more muscular, with a lethal air about him. Rob discarded that strategy almost immediately. His resigned look showed in his drooped shoulders and sagging jaw.

"Why did you go to see Sandra Stanfield?"

"What's wrong with a friend going to visit a friend in the hospital?"

"How close a friend is she?" Ian closed the gap between them.

Rob shrank back. "I work part-time at the library, and she's been helping me."

"With what?"

Anna took in the cramped space Rob called an apartment. Stacks of books were scattered about the floor. A scarred card table with one fire-engine-red chair sat by the only window. Papers littered the red top, a computer in the midst of them. "Are you the person my sister has been assisting with his dissertation?"

"Yes. We were supposed to meet at the library the next morning. I waited for two hours. I'm afraid I made a scene when she didn't show up. Later, I found out she was in the hospital. I felt bad about my display at the library."

"Is that why you came to visit her?" Ian's question drew Rob's attention back to him.

"I suppose." The man shrugged, putting some space between him and Ian.

Ian pursued him and thrust his face into Rob's. "You suppose? You don't know?"

"I visited her because we fought the last time I saw her. She kept breaking our—appointments." Raking his hand across his brow, which was drenched in sweat, he tried to move away.

Ian wouldn't let him. He blocked his escape. "Appointments? Or dates?" His questions sliced like the steel edge of a sword.

Rob gulped, his features ashen. "We weren't dating."

"But you wanted to be?"

The slump to his shoulders became more pronounced. "Yes, but she was seeing someone else."

"Who?"

"I don't know."

"Come on. You're telling me you didn't know the identity of the man who was taking Sandra away from you?"

"I tried to find out." Rob gulped again, color flushing back into his cheeks. "Once I followed Sandra, but—" Uncertainty entered his gaze.

"But what?"

"I don't know. It was the strangest thing. One minute I was watching Sandra go into the park, the next I fell asleep. When I woke up it was dark, and she was nowhere to be seen."

Anna walked to the card table and fingered the pages of an open book. People flashed across her mind like a strobe light. Then suddenly her sister's laughing face filled her thoughts. Anna saw Sandra smile down at Rob, point to something in the book, then to the computer screen. Rob looked up at Sandra, and the love Anna glimpsed in his eyes took her breath away.

Anna backed away from the card table. Rob's emotions buried her in his suffering. "Let's go, Ian."

She strode to the door, not bothering to glance back to see if he was coming with her. She needed to get out of the apartment. Suddenly she felt not only Rob's emotions but Sandra's—her loneliness, her need to feel special, her awkwardness around men.

Out in the hall, Anna didn't stop. She hurried toward the stairs. When Ian halted her progress and swung her around, she almost lost her balance and had to grab the balustrade to keep from falling.

"What happened in there? Did you get a vision?"

"Yes." Panic swelled her chest, causing her voice to be breathless.

"Then why did you run? You need to go with it to the end."

"I can't do this." She wrenched her arm from his grasp and pounded down the wooden stairs.

For a few seconds silence followed her, then she heard Ian's heavy footsteps behind her. The sound pulsated with anger.

"Wait, Anna."

"No," she tossed back over her shoulder and kept going.

When she hit the first flight of stairs she picked up her pace, flying down the steps two at a time. Outside she finally stopped on the sidewalk, dragging cool air into her lungs. Still, panic gripped her so tightly her chest constricted with each breath she took.

"What the hell happened in there?" Ian planted himself in front of her.

"I felt Sandra. She spent a lot of time in Rob's apartment. It took me by surprise. I knew she was helping a graduate student with his paper, but I didn't know who. Why didn't I know who? I should have been able to tell you about Rob Alexander. I should have known." Anger at herself tangled with her panic, making her feel trapped again, as though she were back in apartment 3B.

"Did you sense anything about the killer?"

Anna blinked. "No, just Sandra's desperation to be loved."

"He would have used that. He would hone in on a person's weakness."

"You sound as if you've met this man."

"I know his type. Predators."

"He's playing a game."

"A deadly game."

***

In the lobby of the large hotel he checked out the women milling about. This would be fun. He thought of the cliché about taking candy from a baby and laughed. Yes, he had lots of delicious pieces of chocolate to pick from. So many—not enough time to sample all, but he would make his point this evening.

A tall, voluptuous woman strode toward the bank of elevators. He rose and followed. Slipping inside at the last second, he leaned back against the mirrored wall.

She stared at the lighted buttons, ignoring him. He stared at her. Apprehension tugged at her composure. Her gaze skidded to him, then back to the panel. As they passed the floors, dings sounded in the silence. Her hand hovered several inches from the red alarm knob.

Anticipation bubbled up in him like the fountain of youth. He already felt invigorated with her life force.

The elevator came to a stop on her floor, and the doors swished opened. She rushed out. He pursued her. Down the hall. Her footsteps quickened. A glance back at him. He smiled and sent a message of calmness to her.

Suddenly her pace slowed, and she turned to face him with her key in her hand. Her beautiful features eased into a sensual greeting, with her full lips puckered, her eyes half-closed. She thrust her key into his grasp and allowed him to open her door.

Stepping inside her room, she dropped her purse at

her feet and offered herself.

Yep, like taking candy from a baby, he thought as he kicked the door shut and closed the short distance between them. He clasped her head, his energy immediately flowing into her to ensnare hers. When he pressed his lips to hers, he sucked her life from her, its tingling waves fusing with his. She arched, took a last breath, then slumped to the floor in minutes.

Without a backward glance he left the room and walked to the next one. He laid his hand on the wood of the door and visualized the occupants. A husband and wife. He moved on. At the next room he saw in his mind a lone woman, getting ready for bed.

He knocked.

Twelve

"Ian! Look at this!" Anna quaked as she handed Ian the front section of the newspaper. "It's him!"

He read the headlines then the story and swore.

"He killed ten women in one hotel, mostly on one floor last night. It's got to be him. No forced entry. No sign of how all the women died," Anna said.

"I can't believe he's moved on."

"Why? You said he doesn't stay long in any one place."

"But he wanted—" Ian crushed the paper in his grasp. "Me."

"Yes, you."

"Because you're here, he's giving up on me. You need to go to Chicago."

"No, that's what he wants."

"Do you honestly think I'm that important to him? He's moved on. You've got to stop him."

"No. My best bet is here."

"Not if he isn't here." She gestured toward the paper still balled in his hand. "I can't let any more women die because you won't leave me to pursue him. I have enough guilt over Sandra."

"He's playing a game. I won't participate."

"You may not have a choice."

"Didn't you once tell me that we always have choices?"

Anna stood, her hands fisted at her sides. She directed

her anger at the situation, at him. "Well, my choice at the moment is to go to class—alone."

"No. Not acceptable."

Her glare drilled into him. He met it with a calm facade that fueled her anger even more. "I can ask you to leave."

"Yes, you can."

"But you wouldn't go?"

He smiled, but a sadness touched his eyes. "What do you think?"

"This is my house, and there are laws you must abide by."

Instead of saying anything, Ian pushed to his feet, let the wadded paper fall to the kitchen table, and shoved his chair in. "Ready?"

Anna bit her bottom lip to keep from screaming. How could the man be so reserved? Snatching up her purse, she stomped toward the front door. She wanted her life back. She wanted Ian, and he hadn't touched her in several days. Damn the man for making her feel!

***

"There's been another incident, this time in Dallas," Terri said the second Ian came on the phone.

A savage curse exploded from his lips.

"You've got to do something. He's taunting us—you."

"What do you want me to do? I'm working with Anna, but ever since the bombing there's been a barrier between us. I can't get past it."

"Caused by you or her?"

"Both."

"He may be gone. This is two cities in three days. He's probably changed his appearance by now. He certainly has enough energy to make the transformation. In fact, he has enough energy reserve to transform many times over."

"I'm starting to wonder if he wants me to find him.

He's become so blatant."

"A showdown?"

"What other thrill can give him such a high? He's done everything else short of shouting our existence from a rooftop."

"You need to check on this latest series of deaths."

Ian released a long sigh. "I know. But what about Anna?"

"I'll look after her."

"And Sandra? You can't do both. And we don't have time to bring anyone else in that I would trust."

"I'll do whatever you think is best. With his ability to change appearances, the Chameleon is probably no longer interested in Sandra, especially if he's moved on. For that matter, if he's moved on, Anna will be safe, too. He hasn't revisited a city yet. Too many places he can go."

"I don't know, Terri. Something is wrong here."

"Is that the Hawk talking, or Ian? I've seen how you look at Anna. There's a chemistry between you. Is it interfering with your judgment?"

The sound of footsteps coming down the stairs warned him Anna was awake. "I have to go. I'll let you know what I decide."

"Don't take too long. We don't have time to waste."

He replaced the receiver in its cradle, tracing his finger along its slim, forest green surface. For one of the few times in his life he didn't know what to do. He didn't want to leave Anna alone, and yet his duty demanded he did. If the Chameleon was gone, he needed to follow his trail. Staying in Lexington wouldn't accomplish anything, and more women would die.

"Who was that on the phone?" Anna asked, coming into the kitchen and heading for the pot of coffee.

"Terri."

She swirled about. "Is something wrong with Sandra?"

"No. There hasn't been any change." Ian paced from one end of the room to the other. "But there has been another series of murders, in Dallas this time."

With her hands shaking she finished pouring her coffee, some of it sloshing over the side of the mug. She stared at the brown liquid on the white tiled counter. Her shoulders sagged as she seemed to curl in on herself. "I feel responsible."

"Why? You had nothing to do with it."

His words, spoken vehemently, lashed out at her. The frayed bits of his anger nailed her with his frustration and guilt. "You should have gone to Chicago. You didn't because of me."

"I didn't because I believed I was doing the right thing by staying here."

"Are you going to Dallas?"

"Yes. I can't ignore this change in his MO."

"Will you come back?" she asked before she had time to decide whether or not she wanted to hear the answer.

The question hung in the air between them. He stopped pacing. As though paralyzed, he stared at her from across the room. Each beat of her heart enhanced her awareness of him. She imagined his heart thudding in the same, slow rhythm.

"I don't know."

"So this is good-bye."

"Yes. I have a duty." He moved with such quick speed that suddenly Anna found herself being hauled against him, her mouth crushed beneath his. "No, Anna. I can't ignore what's happened between us."

He cradled her head in his hands. The probing edges of his mind fanned outward, nibbling at hers. She opened her thoughts to him, welcoming his invasion. Her spirit entwined with his, meshing as one, as if they had mated. When he pulled back, releasing his hold, what fulfillment she'd experienced evaporated like the last rays of the sun before night fell.

"Please call me and let me know what's happening in Dallas or wherever you end up."

"For the time being, Terri is staying here with Sandra. If your sister wakes up, she may still be able to help us."

"Thank you for keeping Terri with Sandra."

"I want you to keep her informed of your whereabouts. Before I leave, we'll set up a schedule for you to check in with her. Promise me you won't be alone with anyone, even someone you consider a friend."

She smiled, the corners of her mouth trembling. "I won't. I've seen enough suspense movies to know the folly in that. If it'll make you feel better, I'll even stay with Terri and Sandra at night."

The grin that accompanied his touch was all the answer she needed. She went into his embrace again, afraid this might be the last time she saw him. She knew he was holding back the complete truth, but she trusted him to keep her safe. It was her heart she wasn't sure she trusted him with.

***

With a large cup of coffee to fortify her, Anna sat at her kitchen table and jotted down another name. She knew more men than she had originally thought. The list was long, and she kept thinking of more to add as she went through her day. Of course, the killer very likely wasn't someone she knew, but she couldn't stand to be idle. Ian had been gone only thirty-six hours, and she already missed him. In the past couple of weeks he'd become a part of her life, more than was safe for her peace of mind. Because he would leave her broken-hearted. She knew that as well as she knew her name. He cared about others but at a distance. Just the fact there were secrets surrounding him proved to her that he could never trust another enough to allow her completely into his life. And that was the only way she would have a relationship.

She pulled out the piece of paper with a list of fifteen names on it. After talking with Sandra's co-workers and friends, these were all the men she could think of with whom Sandra was more than occasionally acquainted. She'd decided men like the grocer and the paperboy wouldn't be on the list of suspects. Sandra wouldn't go to bed with just anyone.

Comparing the rosters revealed only five duplicate names, which might mean something but probably didn't. She and her sister didn't move in the same circles. The two lists only reconfirmed that they lived very different lives although physically only a few miles apart. Sad. If she got a second chance with Sandra, that would change.

When the doorbell rang, Anna jumped, dropping her pencil. Should she ignore the person on her front porch? *Trust no one.* Since Ian had left, she'd stayed at home when she wasn't at the long-term care facility with her sister and Terri or teaching her classes. She hadn't even kept her office hours yesterday, which was most unusual for her. One student had commented on that in class this morning.

The closed drapes darkened her normally bright house. She thrived on sunlight and hated feeling like a hermit living in a cave.

The doorbell chimed again.

She chewed on her lower lip and tried to decide what to do. It wouldn't hurt to at least see who was at the door. No one needed to know she was at home. Curiosity lured her toward the entry hall. Just a look through the peephole.

"Anna, it's Ian." A pounding sound accompanied the words.

She rushed to the door and thrust it open. She fell into Ian's arms. He'd come back. In the dark recesses of her mind, she'd feared she would never see him again.

"What did you find out?" she asked, pulling him into her house.

"Not much, I'm afraid."

She strode into the living room, gesturing for him to sit on the couch as she pulled open the curtains. Sunlight flooded the room and warmed her insides. Everything was right with the world if, for a few moments, she pretended there wasn't a killer murdering women and Sandra was fine.

When she curled up next to Ian on the couch, she touched his face, relishing the rough texture of his jaw, covered in a day old beard. "Tell me about Dallas."

He rubbed his hand where hers had touched. "Sorry. I must look a sight. All I could think about was getting back here to you."

That declaration sent her heart soaring. "You look wonderful to me."

He cupped her chin and brought her closer to him, his lips brushing across hers. "You stole my line—my heart."

***

"Terri, this is Ian."

Terri shifted the phone to the other ear. "Where are you?"

"At the Dallas airport. I should be back in Lexington in a few hours."

"Did you discover anything?"

"The Chameleon has been busy. He hit two hotels in Dallas. I just finished up with the second scene. He couldn't have been gone more than a few hours. Someone found a dead woman in an elevator. After what happened at the airport hotel, the authorities did a room-to-room check. Four more women were dead."

"But no sign of the Chameleon."

"The frustrating part is, with all the energy he's

gathering, he's discarding appearances like a person does clothes. The description from the witnesses at both hotels was different." Ian released a pent up breath. "How's Anna?"

"She left here a while ago. She was going to her class then straight home. She called to let me know she got home and was going to stay put."

"I'm heading to her house as soon as I get in. This whole affair is puzzling. He's never left behind witnesses before. But people at both hotels saw the man they think is responsible."

"Have the Circle perfected that monitor yet?"

"Almost. It certainly will make my job easier. I know I have to be in the same area as one of us to detect a Cintarian, but it will help. I get the feeling the Chameleon has been near, but whenever I probe a person's mind I sense nothing unusual."

"He's powerful. He's gathered a lot of energy. He can mask himself better than most. I don't know why we didn't come up with a monitor sooner."

"The Circle didn't want there to be any way for someone to detect a Cintarian. Remember, some in the Circle were our leaders during the Dark Period when so many of us were destroyed in the Hunt."

"And we haven't had anyone so blatantly trying to expose us as the Chameleon is, not even his father. Doesn't he realize it will hurt him, too?"

"I don't think he cares anymore. He's gotten a taste of what unlimited energy can do, and he wants it no matter who it harms. I need to go. They're announcing my flight. See you soon."

***

"I never thought I would fall in love," Ian said, drawing Anna into his embrace. "While I was in Dallas, all I could think about was you and getting back to you."

"I don't know what to say. I missed you so much. I--" Anna swallowed her words, unable to voice aloud her feelings.

He covered her mouth with the tips of his fingers. "You don't have to say anything." Framing her face, he lowered his head toward hers, assaulting her senses with his gentle possession. Soft. Tender.

Then all of a sudden his mouth came down on hers in a bruising ownership, driving her back on the couch. Something wasn't right. Energy pushed at the walls of her mind, demanding entrance.

She managed to twist her head to the side. "Ian?"

He laughed, a sound that grated on her senses like a discordant musical note. "I thought you wanted me."

His body pressed into hers, making each breath she took difficult. The pressure in her lungs ignited a slow burn that spread throughout her body. "I did." She looked into his dark eyes, and none of his previous warmth was evident. Again the feeling that something wasn't right assailed her. "I do. But not like this."

He eased off her, a gleam entering his eyes. "I'm sorry. All I thought about was you and making love to you. I got carried away. Forgive me."

His slanted look held the warmth she was accustomed to. Her tension subsided. Sitting up, she straightened her shirt and said, "There's nothing to forgive. I was just surprised."

He rose and offered her his hand. "Then let's begin again and do it properly this time."

Anna placed her palm over his, expecting to feel the familiar zip of energy flow into her. She didn't. Disappointed, she allowed him to draw her to her feet, deciding this whole situation was taking more of a toll than they had thought.

He pulled her toward her bedroom, his gaze connected to hers as though he'd roped her to him. The king-sized bed beckoned. Eager to renew that feeling of safety she experienced in his arms, she lay down and opened hers wide for him. He came down onto her, one of his legs thrown over hers.

Combing her hair back, he held her head, his gaze boring into her with an intensity that sought to dominate. "You're mine now, Anna. No one can come between us."

Her alarm clamored with the fiery force behind his words. She struggled to move from beneath him. His grip tightened about her, a band across her chest that again threatened to crush the air from her lungs.

"Ian, let me up!"

His laughter drenched her with mounting fear. "I've wanted you like this for a long time."

She tried to twist away, but he mashed her against the bedding, covering her completely with his body. With one hand, he clenched hers over her head and stared down at her. The gleam in his eyes held no warmth now, but a dark glint that drilled through her.

"You're not Ian."

"I always thought you were too clever. No, I'm not Ian."

"But how?" Fear hammered against her chest as though a part of her heartbeat.

The sound of his laughter ricocheted against the walls of her mind. "Let me demonstrate my power."

Before her eyes Anna saw his features shift, melting and blending into different ones. *No, this isn't possible!*

"Yes, my dear, it is very possible. I do it all the time. I'm whoever I want to be."

She blinked, her gaze riveted to the image of David. "Who are you? What are you?"

"You know me as David Pierce. My people know me as the Chameleon. I belong to a race of people far superior to humans. In fact, your lover is one of us. How else do you think he knows so much about me and has been fairly successful in tracking me?"

"You're an alien?" She closed her eyes for a few seconds, sure that when she opened them again she would awaken from this horrible nightmare. There was no such things as aliens, except in movies and books.

"Alien? I've lived on Earth longer than you. We were here at the beginning when my people came from Cintar."

"Where's David? What have you done with him?"

"Nothing. I am David. I've enjoyed playing that role, but it's time to move on—after I take care of Ian once and for all."

Her fear took on a new dimension. "He's not here."

"I know. I lured him to Dallas. But he will be back. In fact, he's on his way now. I've toyed with him long enough. Baiting him has lost its appeal."

"I don't understand. Why me?"

"You have a great psychic power that will enhance mine. And I want to take something away from Ian that means a lot to him."

"He was only my bodyguard."

His hideous laughter bombarded her. "Yeah, he guarded your body."

Ian was on his way. Maybe she could distract David long enough for him to arrive. "You said my psychic power can enhance yours. How?"

"To sustain ourselves, we use energy generated by a person. Usually a Cintarian keeps his same body for a generation or so and doesn't require much energy from a human. Just enough to keep himself healthy, aging at a slow rate, and his powers sharp."

"So that's what you did to Sandra. You drained her?"

"Yes, and she was a challenge. Like you will be."

"Why do you kill your victims?"

"Why not? I don't care about the human race, and the

more energy I can get from you, the better I am. My race has decided to influence this world from afar. They should be ruling it. But they won't listen to me, so I decided to do something about it. I'm tired of watching humans. I want to be in the middle, controlling everything."

The cold truth to his words chilled her as though he'd instantly frozen her.

"You know, my dear, I rather liked you. You were entertaining for a while." He placed his free hand on her head. "But now it's time to implement the next step in my plan."

"What?" Tingling waves of energy surged through his fingertips, spreading into her mind.

"When my father died, he'd been imprisoned by the Cintarians for hundreds of years. He wasted away with no means of rejuvenating his energy. That's how they deal with rogues. Ian was the one who brought my father in, as well as my older brother. I will never forgive him for their deaths." Angry lines creased his forehead and slashed his mouth.

Oh, God, he's going to kill Ian after me! He'd laid a trap with her as the bait. In a last burst of energy, Anna sent out a message to Ian to stay away, praying that he received and heeded it.

David increased his grip on her, a fierce expression contorting his features. "You're wasting your time. He'll come because you're in danger."

The flow of energy expanded as David battered at her mental barriers. She turned her concentration on protecting herself. She would fight him until nothing was left. Pulling back into a deep corner of her mind, she drew in on herself, erecting a high blockade. He scaled the obstacles she threw at him, consuming her essence as he neared her core. Withstanding his pounding force, she mentally curled into a tight ball and shielded her inner spirit. She wouldn't surrender. She wouldn't give him any more fuel for his evilness.

The thought of her sacred place nourished her hope. *This is your way out when things get too much for you. All you have to do is walk through that gate. You control it. You'll be safe.* Ian's remembered words soothed the fear that had dug its talons in deep. If she could leave the garden by the gate, she could also go there now.

Visualizing her haven, Anna sought refuge in the walled garden as David continued to pummel her defenses. With little energy left, she lay on the cool grass by the fountain. The sun caressed her face, and the bubbling sound of the water consoled her waning spirit. She was dying, but in her death there would be a part of her he would never have, her core.

***

Stay away!

The plea invaded Ian's mind causing him to falter. He grasped onto a car in the parking lot at the Lexington airport to steady himself. For a few seconds the trembling in his legs threatened to incapacitate him. Sucking in a deep breath of the spring air, he sent his mind outward, searching for the source of the urgent message.

In his thoughts he saw Anna pinned beneath the Chameleon, struggling to stay alive. He cried out his rage, the sound carrying on the wind as if he was a warrior preparing to go into battle. Strength surged through him. He grew stronger with each step nearer to his car.

An eternity later he arrived at Anna's house, slamming on the brakes and racing toward the front door. He tried the knob. It was locked. With all his power he kicked at the door until the wood frame shattered. Shoving his way inside, he hurried toward the bedroom, praying he wasn't too late to save her.

When he burst into the room, David glanced back at

him as he climbed off Anna who lay unconscious on the bed, her face pale.

"No!" Ian shouted.

David smiled. "I'm afraid yes. She was quite delicious and fulfilling."

A part of Ian wanted to shut down and mourn Anna. But the part of him that had been driven over the years to track down the Chameleon bolstered his inner spirit and eased the turmoil reeling in his mind.

"She will be the last human you'll ever have." Ian knew he wouldn't take the Chameleon as a prisoner.

David perfected a nonchalant stance, looking bored. "And you think you'll be able to stop me? Anna was a powerful psychic. Her energy is strong. In fact, the best I've ever had. I'm not afraid to enjoy our human brethren to the fullness."

Ian compressed his spirit into a ball of light and soared above his physical body into a plane where only Cintarians could exist. Facing the wall of darkness, he prepared himself to fight the Chameleon until only one of them was left. Power, strong and steady, emanated from the Chameleon's shadow. Its blast propelled Ian back.

Gathering every ounce of energy he had, Ian stood his ground, marshaling his resources to obliterate his foe once and for all. For a few seconds rage blocked his concentration. He viewed Anna, eyes closed and lying limp on her bed. He stamped down the anger blocking him from what he must do and focused his mind into a narrow beam of light that shot out from his core.

The Chameleon staggered back, his dark glow dimming.

Ian drew on his reserve, gathering his forces to strike again. A mind-shattering current flew from the center of the blackness, knocking him back. Another stream of energy came at Ian before he could muster his defenses.

Locking on Ian, the Chameleon began to drain him.
He was too strong. Ian needed to refortify himself.
But where?

Anna's walled garden. The thought popped into his mind, enticing him there. He withdrew into her sacred place where everything in the outside world would be shut out unless Anna wanted it.

When he saw her lying on the grass by the fountain, his heart stopped beating for a few seconds. In a blink he was at her side, kneeling down next to her and gathering her into his arms. She smiled up at him.

"You came." She reached up and traced his mouth with the tips of her fingers, soft, only a whisper against his skin.

Her voice, as soft as her touch, ripped at all the barriers he'd placed around his emotions. Once and for all he lay bare before her.

"Of course," he choked out, his own voice as weak as hers.

"You must stop him." Her eyes drifted closed.

"I'm trying, but he's gathered a lot energy in the past few weeks."

"He didn't get—" she swallowed hard, her gaze linked with his, "all mine. Take it. Use it to destroy him."

"I can't. It could kill you."

"I'm already gone, Ian. I can't get back."

"There's always hope. Sandra's still alive."

"She's not living. She's a shell. I don't want that." Her voice rose, the exertion causing her to cough. "I would rather die. Please."

"Don't ask me to do that. I'll find another way to defeat him." His vision blurred, her beautiful features shimmering. "I love you. I can't do it."

"You must." Tears rolled down her face. "I love you, Ian. You have a chance. I don't."

Ian threw back his head, the sun streaming down to caress his face in warmth. Inside he felt so cold that nothing would ever heat him again. He yelled his frustration, cursing the Chameleon and cursing the Fates. He had to leave before he did what she asked. He started to rise.

"Please, Ian."

Her soft, husky voice enticed him back. The beseeching look in her eyes clawed at his defenses.

"It's all I ask."

Her smile sliced through the ice that had enveloped him. He settled back down next to her and cradled her head between his hands. Her gaze riveted to his.

"I love you. I always will, Ian. You taught me to believe in myself."

Tears slipped down his face. "I'll never forget you in all the years I live."

He closed his eyes and pushed his life force into her, harvesting what energy she had left. Even though she'd wanted him to take it all, he couldn't kill her. He'd never killed a human by draining them completely of their life force, and he wouldn't start with Anna. He flowed back out of her, leaving behind a small glimmer of life.

Her limp, almost spiritless, body lay in his arms. He pressed her against his beating heart, part of himself dying as she was. "I won't let your sacrifice be in vain, Anna. I promise."

He kissed her dry, cool lips, then placed her gently on the grass. Scanning her walled garden, he inhaled a deep breath of the flower-scented air. A butterfly lit on the fountain, fanned its wings then took off again. A cardinal's chirp vied with the sound of water flowing from the stone statue of an angel.

A myriad of emotions from anger to love welled up inside him, overwhelming him with years of holding them at bay. He experienced it all in that moment and realized that after this he would never feel again. He wouldn't allow himself to.

He pushed to his feet and glanced one more time down at Anna, lying peacefully, her serene features cast in alabaster like a marble sculpture. "Good-bye, my love."

His spirit poured through the gate, ready to finish what he had started, for Anna. He hurled a stream of energy at the Chameleon before his enemy even realized Ian had resumed the battle.

The dark ball swayed, returning fire after a few seconds. Ian threw up a shield to protect himself from the malignancy threatening to engulf him. Rivers of energy surged, and sparks of lightning flashed. Ian cast everything he had at the Chameleon, determined to stand his ground until there was nothing left in him.

His armor buckled and wavered under the Chameleon's steady flow. He staggered back. Visions of Anna filled his thoughts, and he stiffened his resolve. From deep within he drew on his reserve and flung his total being at the Chameleon. He merged with the blackness, his light slowly eroding the gloom. The sphere around Ian trembled as though a deadly bomb had exploded. When the last ray of dark faded, a flare of white-hot energy ignited and burned.

Ian slumped forward, drained and exhausted. The brightness of his surroundings and the pain ripping at his insides told him the Chameleon was gone for good. He should have been elated, but memories of Anna plagued him. Grief cloaked him, whisking away any pleasure he should have at finally defeating his enemy. Without Anna what did he have? Too late he'd discovered how much she meant to him.

***

When Ian regained his strength, and the pain from a Cintarian's death had subsided, he materialized in Anna's bedroom. It took a few seconds for him to orient himself to his surroundings. Stumbling to the bed, he collapsed next to her, emotions jamming in his throat. He pulled her into his arms and held her against him, feeling the faint thud of her beating heart. She was alive—barely.

Everything inside him screamed at the injustice. If he could, he would destroy the Chameleon all over again. He would feel the excruciating pain of his death a thousand times over to save Anna.

Exhausted, he cradled her, letting his mind drift into a void where nothing existed. Its healing powers began to work their magic on him while something inside him died. Without Anna, what would he have?

As he floated in the soothing dark, he tried to imagine his life without her. Empty like the void he was in.

Slowly his strength returned, and he retreated from the nothingness, physically repaired, but emotionally marred. He didn't want to feel. It hurt too much. Why hadn't he been able to stop this from happening?

Darkness bathed the bedroom. He felt the gentle rise and fall of Anna's chest as she breathed. Her jasmine scent enveloped him in memories of them entwined together on this very bed, with him making love to her body as well as her mind. He wanted that back. He wanted her *back*.

He shot up in bed. He knew how to accomplish that. Pushing to his feet, he stood staring down at her. He would have to get the Circle's permission. Healing a human through a mind merge hadn't been done since the Dark Period thousands of years before. But it might be possible to bring her back. He had to try. It was his only hope.

He dialed the long-term care facility. "Terri, the Chameleon's dead."

"I felt his death."

"I need you to come to Anna's house and watch over

her until I get back."

"Where are you going?"

"To the Mountain to put a request before the Circle."

"The Chameleon got to Anna?"

"She's in a deep coma, like Sandra. I want to try to heal both her and her sister with a mind merge."

"They won't let you. It's too dangerous, and it might not work."

"I have to try. I'm hoping I can persuade them." He heard the fervent tone in his voice and prayed he could pull off the impossible.

"I'll be there in twenty minutes."

When Ian hung up, he sat again on the bed and took Anna's hand in his. "When I come back, I'll join you in your garden, and we will leave it together."

***

"If Anna hadn't protected some of her energy, the Chameleon would have used it against me and won. If she hadn't insisted I take the last bit of her energy, I don't know that I could have defeated the Chameleon. Simply put, Anna protected us, and because of that she's in a deeper coma."

The hardness of the chair Ian sat on reminded him of the strict rules that governed the Cintarians on Earth. He scanned the familiar faces of the Circle. Their displeasure at his request carved deep lines of grim determination into their features.

"We appreciate the sacrifices this human made for us, but you can't heal her. It is dangerous. It is forbidden," his uncle said, finally breaking the silence that clung to the air like moisture.

"I'm willing to risk the danger for Anna. Why is it forbidden?"

"It has been for thousands of years."

"That's not good enough for me."

"Well, it will have to do, son. Besides, I don't know that you can bring her back. From what you've told us, she is barely hanging on."

"Because of me—*us.*" Ian's anger rose and filled each word he spoke. "Anna Stanfield is part Cintarian. She has a powerful psychic ability, powerful enough to hold off the Chameleon and allow herself time to escape to her sacred place. He couldn't breach her walled garden." He searched the face of each member of the Circle, wishing he could delve beneath their neutral expressions. "Why are we turning away from our own?"

Dolphin leaned forward. "She is part human. An outsider, not one of us."

"I don't accept that answer any longer."

"You're allowing your emotions to rule you. Have you not learned the lessons we learned long ago about letting our feelings be our guide? It nearly destroyed our race."

"And ignoring our emotions will also destroy us. We exist. That is all. The joy has gone out of our lives since the Dark Period. I think I would prefer that time to now. At least then I would know I am alive."

His uncle stood, his age showing in his slow movements. "We cannot change on your whim a law that has governed us for so long. You are the Protector. You above all must obey our laws."

The penetrating intensity of his uncle's gaze sliced through him, bringing to the forefront Ian's dilemma. If he followed the Cintarian laws, Anna would die. If he didn't, he would be betraying his people as the one person responsible for protecting them from the outside world. How could he turn his back on his race? How could he let Anna go?

"We are a dying race. We must preserve what little we have," his uncle said.

"We aren't a dying race. Many among the humans

have our blood running through their veins. Our genes are a part of them. We will always live on in them."

"It is not the same," Dolphin said with a wave of her hand.

"You live here at the top of this mountain. When was the last time you walked among the humans, lived among them? You've isolated yourselves from your human relations and only go among them when you need their energy to sustain you."

The white-haired woman rose. "This is enough. The Circle has spoken. Anna Stanfield shall remain as she is. We can't risk her recovering and telling of our existence. Can you imagine the chaos that would occur if the humans knew we lived among them and influenced some of their decisions?"

Ian drew himself up straight, the emotions he was supposed to deny churning his stomach. He had lost. Anna had lost.

Thirteen

"Thank you for watching over Anna while I was gone," Ian said as he entered her bedroom.

Terri looked up from the magazine she was flipping through. "How did it go? What did the Circle say?"

"No."

Her hopeful expression fell. "I'm so sorry. But they have good reason for feeling the way they do."

"The Dark Period was thousands of years ago. Times change. We need to change, too."

"Have you forgotten the ones we lost?"

"No, but the humans weren't ready for the truth then. Maybe some are now. I'm not saying we should proclaim our existence to the whole world."

"Only to Anna?"

He sank down on the bed next to Anna. "Frankly that's all I care about. I owe her my life, and much more."

"What are you going to do?" Terri's brow wrinkled in a deep frown as she dropped the magazine on the end table beside her.

"Say good-bye to her. Take the rest of her energy so she may die as she requested. I can do that much for her at least."

"You've never done that, Ian. That may be dangerous for you. Once a Cintarian experiences—"

He held up his hand to stop her words. "I know the lure of totally taking a human's life force. If I become a rogue, you can hunt me down."

"Don't joke about it."

"I'm not. But I'm going to do this for Anna. She didn't want to live in a vegetative state."

"Do you want me to stay?"

"No. I want to be alone with her this last time."

Terri stood and headed for the door. Glancing back over her shoulder, she offered him a faint smile. "You're the Protector for the Cintarians because you do such a good job. Keep that in mind. Perhaps that will help you through what you must do."

Ian stretched out next to Anna on the bed and grasped her hand. Her faint pulse asserted she was alive. If you called living in a deep coma—never smiling, laughing, enjoying life again—being alive.

He turned, facing her, and gathered her close. When he appeared in her walled garden, he found her as he'd left her, lying next to the fountain on the lush green grass. He watched her for a moment, relishing her beauty. As he strode to her, a tightness in his throat made each breath difficult. He eased down onto the ledge of the fountain next to her, resting his elbows on his knees and clasping his hands.

How can I be responsible for her death?

The question ran through his mind over and over, producing a pressure in his chest that was both suffocating and searing. For hundreds of years he'd been the Protector. Ever since he was a child, he'd been groomed to follow in his father's footsteps and guard his race from the outside world.

How can I turn my back on the past thousands of years?

He didn't have an answer for that question, either. Confusion divided him in half, until he felt as if there were two of him, and the parts were warring with each other.

Leaning down, he traced his finger along Anna's lips, then feathered his own across hers. *Respond, dammit. Live.*

He sat in the grass and dragged her back against him, his arms encircling her. Her faint heart beating against him brought all the conflict he felt to the foreground. He wanted her to live. He couldn't kill her. If he did, he might as well kill himself.

That left only one thing for him to do—defy thousands of years of training and purpose to save Anna. He would have to turn his back on his people.

He clutched her to him and rocked back and forth, wishing there was another way. She deserved to live, even if the Cintarians hunted him down for disobeying an order of the Circle.

With her head between his hands, he closed his eyes and slipped into her mind, merging with her on a level more intimate than mating. His energy entwined with what little she had left and fed it with his life force. They became one in every sense for a few seconds. What was her was him and what was him was her.

As he retreated from her, her strength began to expand, spreading outward from her core to encompass her whole body. With a waning stamina, he managed to leave the walled garden, returning to her bedroom. The last thing he remembered as unconsciousness descended was Anna stirring next to him.

***

With a jolt Anna emerged from the depth of darkness. Sunlight streamed through the open draperies, illuminating her bedroom, not the walled garden. Its brightness chased away the chill of the black void. She shifted and felt someone next to her. Twisting her head, she saw Ian lying beside her, serenity sculpting his features.

Then what he'd done flooded her mind. His essence

flowed through her, bound with hers as though they'd mated on a sphere not possible for humans. He had given her his life force. He had saved her, brought her back from the edge of death.

She laid her hand on his chest and sighed when she felt his heart pounding beneath her palm. Strong, slow.

Collapsing back, she stared at the white ceiling, trying to assimilate everything that had occurred in the past few days. Her head throbbed with her attempt. Massaging her temples, she began to piece together the events that had transpired. Was the Chameleon dead? What had Ian done to bring her back? Who were the Cintarians? The Circle? Was Ian an alien with psychic powers beyond human comprehension? All his past experiences tumbled through her mind so fast that she felt dizzy. And she knew the truth.

Overriding everything was the knowledge that Ian had betrayed his own people to save her.

No! The thought pulled her back down into the darkness. She didn't want to be the cause of such pain for him.

Bolting up, she looked around frantically, trying to decide what to do. At best he would be banished from his people. How could she live knowing that it was her fault? He would grow to hate her over time. She would die hundreds of years before him, leaving him alone, alienated from his race. What would he have then?

How can I undo what he did?

She scrambled to the side of the bed and started to stand. A hand clamped around her arm and hauled her back.

"Where are you going?"

Ian captured her against him. She couldn't look at him. She didn't have an answer.

"How are you feeling?" He tilted her face so he could

peer down at her. "What's going on?"

"Nothing," she squeaked out and realized immediately he could tell she was lying. He knew her as well as she knew herself. She drew in a deep breath, held it for a few seconds, then blew it out. "Why did you go against your people?"

He combed her hair away from her face and stared long and hard at her. "Do I really have to answer that question? You know everything I'm feeling."

"They have been your whole life, Ian. I don't want to be the one who took you away from them."

"For longer than you can imagine I've given myself to the Cintarians. I've put my life on hold for them. I never asked anything in return. When they refused to listen to reason and denied my request to heal you, I couldn't let you go. I tried. I just couldn't. My people live too much in fear. They live in the past. I can't do that any longer."

The constriction in her throat caught her words and held them. Tears crowded her eyes.

"I haven't given up hope they'll see the truth."

"What truth?"

"That we can't turn our backs on our children. We have never openly been a part of our human children's lives. If we are involved, it is from afar."

"You have children?"

He smiled, the crinkles at the sides of his eyes deep. "No. I knew I couldn't father a child and not be a part of his or her life."

"Why do they demand that you stay away?"

"Because during the Dark Period our race was nearly destroyed. Some humans discovered our existence and tried to kill us because they were afraid of us. There are only a little over a thousand of us left from the island."

"Island? The one in your memory that blew up and sank into the ocean?"

"Yes. When we first came to Earth, we lived on that island and only had limited relationships with the humans—when we needed to feed on their life force. Some of us were away when the island was destroyed. A few escaped and made it to the mainland. A lot of Cintarians died the day the island erupted and sank."

Anna rubbed her hand across her forehead to ease the throb behind her eyes. "This is so unbelievable."

"I also think that the Circle—the council that rules us—forbade any humans knowing of our existence, even the children we fathered, because they knew how hard it is emotionally to watch people you love die. After a while you shut down. As a race we have done that anyway. We're involved with humans, but only on an intellectual level."

"And you think they will change their minds?"

"We are a dying race, Anna. Granted it will be another thousand years before we all die out, but we can't reproduce among ourselves. Our women can't have children. The men can only father children with human women. These people are the ones in your race who are psychic, and the more ability a person has, the more Cintarian blood he has."

"Then I'm part Cintarian?" She struggled to sit up and face him. Disbelief mixed with excitement at the prospects.

"Yes. Very much. You have a strong psychic talent."

"Who am I related to? Is he still alive?"

"I don't know. Each Cintarian male handles it differently. Some keep track. Others don't, preferring not to get too attached. We have no records."

"How sad."

"I agree. Because the humans with Cintarian blood will be our only survivors when the last one of us dies. We should be teaching these humans how to deal with their abilities instead of letting them shut them down."

"Or fearing them like I did."

"Most humans with Cintarian blood live longer and are much healthier because of our genes. They have a lot to offer the people of Earth, but they need to be trained properly."

"Are you the only one who feels this way?"

"No. There are others."

"Have you approached the Circle about this?"

"The elders are afraid. My uncle, who sits on the council, knows how I feel, but most of his family was killed during the Dark Period. He has a hard time forgetting."

Anna clasped her legs to her chest and rested her head on her knees. "I want to talk with the Circle. Is that possible?"

Ian's gaze widened. "You?"

"Yes, I have a right to. I have Cintarian blood in me. I need to let them know what I went through as a child, not knowing how to deal with my talents. They need to be responsible for their children."

Ian laughed. "If anyone can convince them, my dear Anna, it will be you. I'll try contacting my uncle, but I don't know if he will respond."

"If he's as smart as his nephew, he will." Anna curled her hand around Ian's neck and dragged him toward her. "You said something about having no children. How do you feel about them?"

His mouth grazed hers. "I could be persuaded by the right woman."

"Mmm. That's sounds interesting." She pulled him down with her and wrapped her arms about him. "Some people have said I can be very persuasive."

Fourteen

Anna scanned the wide vista before her, following the progress of an eagle as it glided on an air current. The sound of the wind coming up from the valley below calmed her tautened nerves. The sight of her chewed fingernails brought a smile to her lips. This might be the most important speech she would ever give, and she wasn't even sure her throat would work. It felt dry as the desert not too far from the Mountain.

"Ready?" Ian came out onto the deck, taking her hand within his. "Remember, I'll be by your side." He laid his other palm over her rounded stomach. "We both are with you."

Terri stood inside the doorway and offered them a smile. "Anna, it's a good sign they have allowed you to come to the Mountain. You are the first human to do so."

"The Circle just misses Ian, and we're a package deal now," Anna quipped, her nerves tightening again as they strode toward the council room.

"True. He has been the Protector for so long they don't know what to do without him. I think they were all surprised to find he went against their wishes. It's forced them to reexamine their thinking."

"And in the year Ian and I have been married, no catastrophes have occurred because Sandra and I know about the Cintarians." Anna thought of her younger sister and the close relationship they now had—all because of

Ian and the second chance he'd given them.

"That has helped, too," Terri said with a twinkle in her eye.

Anna paused at the large double doors with strange symbols carved in the wood. She knew that was the Cintarian language and was just beginning to learn to read it. Her heartbeat roared in her ears. Her lungs seized her breath, contracting her chest.

Ian clasped her shoulders and leaned her back so he could whisper into her ear, "You're the bravest woman I know. That's one of the things I love about you."

She slanted a glance toward him. "What if they send someone after you for breaking their law?"

"They haven't so far. I don't think they will now."

Anna inhaled a deep, fortifying breath and pushed the doors open. She entered the large council room. With her shoulders squared and her chin lifted, she walked to the head of the table where Ian had told her she would stand. A few of the Circle's members nodded a greeting to Ian. The rest stared at them, their expressions unreadable.

The damp moisture of her palms and the dryness of her throat attested to how important this meeting was to Anna. She swallowed several times and began, "I want to thank you for allowing me to come before you and speak on behalf of your human kinfolk of whom I am one." She let her gaze connect with each Cintarian at the round table as Ian had instructed she do.

"When I pledged myself to Ian, I also swore to keep your existence secret. I will continue to do so, but I'm here because I think you should reconsider your stand on the children of your race who are also part human. I was raised with no guidance concerning my psychic talents, and, therefore, my powers were neglected." Anna glanced at Ian next to her. "This past year I've learned a great deal from Ian about my powers. I want others to have that chance. Think of what these people could do for mankind if they had the training you gave your Cintarian children. I want to propose that you not only acknowledge your children born of human women, but that you start an academy for these children to hone their skills."

The silence among the Circle's members was broken. Several whispered among themselves while others, clearly surprised by the suggestion, sat stunned with eyes wide.

Ian clutched her hand and squeezed it.

"I know there's a lot to work out, but the twenty-first century is much different from the Dark Period. I don't propose going public about your existence, but you have ways to control situations and monitor people. Use that if you must, but don't ignore people who have a right to learn of their heritage. A person born of a Cintarian father is as much Cintarian as human. My life would have been much different if I had been able to embrace my talents and use them to help others. Instead, I felt like an outsider and suppressed what should have come naturally to me."

Again the Circle murmured among themselves, a few sending probing thoughts to Anna. She opened her mind to them, letting down her instinctive barriers for them to see her pure intentions.

Ian's uncle rose and waved his hand for quiet. "You have proved to be as brave and persistent as my nephew said you were. You have given us much to think about today. I know some of our people feel the same way. We'll take what you've said under advisement. Thank you for coming."

Anna started to turn and leave but stopped. She cleared her throat and said, "I have one more issue." She waited until she had everyone's attention before continuing, "I realize Ian went against your wishes in healing me and my sister, but my husband took his job as the Protector seriously and gave you hundreds of years of devoted service. I think you should reinstate him as the Protector. You won't find a better one." Again she looked at each member and sent her own silent plea to them.

Ian's uncle smiled. "Now that, I can answer today. We'd already decided to do that. There are too few of us left to turn one like Ian away from his people."

At the door Anna twisted about and added, "Remember what you just said when deciding the fate of your half-human, half-Cintarian children. You have a chance to mold future generations and leave something of yourselves behind when the last Cintarian finally dies."

With her remarks Anna quickly left. She didn't stop until she reached the deck and inhaled deeply of the crisp mountain air. When Ian took her into his arms, she tilted her head back and looked up at him. "It's a good day to be alive, Ian McGregory. I sense they will agree to the academy."

His chuckle washed over her. "And if they don't, you'll be back to ask again."

"You bet I will."

DON'T MISS
SHAUNA MICHAELS'

HOLD ONTO THE NIGHT
ISBN 1-893896-11-0

Geologist Kathleen Dawson is in the South American jungle in search of oil, but her guides are terrified of the Jaguar Man. Kathleen doesn't believe in the mythical shape-shifter who, according to legend, rules the jungle both as beast and man, protecting his territory against the outside world.

Then Kathleen is drugged and awakens to find herself in a cave with a man named Guerriro who claims to be responsible for the Jaguar Man myth. He warns her to leave before it's too late. When morning arrives, Kathleen's back in camp and convinces herself the man and the cave were only a dream. However, her guides find a jaguar's skull on a pole, which is the Jaguar Man's warning that to stay means death. The frightened natives abandon Kathleen.

Stranded in a rainstorm that quickly escalates into a flood, Kathleen fights for her life. She's saved by a black jaguar and again finds herself in Guerriro's cave. But as the days pass, Kathleen begins to wonder if Guerriro, who is both her captor and her savior, is really cursed to live his life as a black jaguar by day and a man by night.

All Kathleen knows for sure is that Guerriro's ensnared her heart, and she'll do anything she can to stay by his side, even if doing so means she must...Hold Onto the Night.

4 1/2 stars Top Pick and nominated for *Romantic Times Magazine's* 2001 Reviewers Choice Award for Best ContempoaryParanormal: *Hold Onto the Night* is a captivating

romance—an action-adventure paranormal with some intrigue. Kathleen is an intelligent heroine and the Jaguar Man is mysteriously wonderful. I highly recommend this to all lovers of shapeshifter romances and anyone else who enjoys something unique.   —Susan Mobley, *Romantic Times*

Available Now from
ImaJinn Books
http://www.imajinnbooks.com
or call 877-625-3592 for a catalog of our books.

ABOUT THE AUTHOR

Shauna Michaels, aka Margaret Ripy and Kit Daley, is a multi-published author with thirty books in the romance genre. She has been writing romances for the past twenty years. She has written for Dell, Silhouette, Kensington, Starlight Writer Publications, and ImaJinn Books. She has mostly written contemporary romances but has done two historicals and one paranormal, *Hold onto the Night.*

Shauna is fortunate enough to be married to the same man for the last twenty-nine years and has one son who is in college right now. She has always felt her husband is her inspiration in life and love and draws on her marriage to write her love stories.

When Shauna isn't working on a book or teaching students with disabilities, she loves to read romances, go to the movies with friends, and travel. She has traveled to many places in the world from South America to Europe. She likes to use these locations in her books. *Hold onto The Night* is placed in a jungle. She had the pleasure of visiting a rain forest in Belize a few years back.

Shauna loves to hear from her readers. You can contact her at P. O. Box 2074, Tulsa, OK, 74101 or you can visit her web site at: http://members.aol.com/APR427/.

TIRED OF MUNDANE ROMANCE?

DARE TO IMAJINN!

If you're looking for something different in your romance, then ImaJinn Books is for you! Sometimes scary, always sexy, our books will bring you romantic adventures with vampires, ghosts, shapeshifters, sorcerers, time-travelers, aliens, reincarnated lovers, and more!

For a complete list of our books, visit our web site at:
http://www.imajinnbooks.com

Or for a copy of our latest catalog, call us toll free at
877-625-3592